Something big growled in the bushes beyond her tent. Kat pulled a 9mm automatic from under her blanket, pointed it at a patch of starlight, and blasted six warning shots into the night sky. . . .

"You got me," a deep voice said, then groaned. Nathan Chatham stumbled out of the bushes, clutching his chest with the hokey drama of a bad actor. "Right through the heart." He sank to the ground, rolled over, and flopped both arms out.

Stunned, she stared at him openmouthed. Laughter was her first impulse, but she was annoyed that he'd tried to scare her. The fact that he was wearing nothing but low-slung leather breeches and moccasins made her pulse skitter. She grabbed the coat hanger with the roasting hot dog and smacked him across the stomach. He yelped as the hot wire hit his skin, but not one furious curse escaped his lips as he quickly stood up. *A gentleman*, she marveled.

"You little hellion. I suppose I deserved that," he said gruffly.

"You know you did." She sniffed a pungent burnt odor. So did he.

"I'm singed," he said, his eyes never leaving hers. "My pelt's worthless now."

"It was worthless before," she murmured, smiling. "Want some ointment?"

"Nope." He grabbed the hot dog and ate it quickly. "I want you, Kat Woman. . . ."

WHAT ARE *LOVESWEPT* ROMANCES?

They are stories of true romance and touching emotion. We believe those two very important ingredients are constants in our highly sensual and very believable stories in the *LOVESWEPT* line. Our goal is to give you, the reader, stories of consistently high quality that may sometimes make you laugh, sometimes make you cry, but are always fresh and creative and contain many delightful surprises within their pages.

Most romance fans read an enormous number of books. Those they truly love, they keep. Others may be traded with friends and soon forgotten. We hope that each *LOVESWEPT* romance will be a treasure—a "keeper." We will always try to publish

LOVE STORIES YOU'LL NEVER FORGET
BY AUTHORS YOU'LL ALWAYS REMEMBER

The Editors

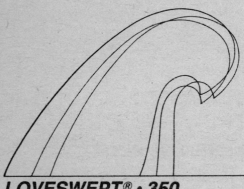

LOVESWEPT® • 350

Deborah Smith
The Cherokee Trilogy: Kat's Tale

 BANTAM BOOKS
NEW YORK • TORONTO • LONDON • SYDNEY • AUCKLAND

KAT'S TALE

A Bantam Book / September 1989

*LOVESWEPT® and the wave device are registered
trademarks of Bantam Books, a division of
Bantam Doubleday Dell Publishing Group, Inc.
Registered in U.S. Patent
and Trademark Office and elsewhere.*

*If you would be interested in receiving protective vinyl
covers for your Loveswept books, please write to this address
for information:*

*Loveswept
Bantam Books
P.O. Box 985
Hicksville, NY 11802*

ISBN 0-553-22020-9

Published simultaneously in the United States and Canada

Bantam Books are published by Bantam Books, a division
of Bantam Doubleday Dell Publishing Group, Inc. Its trademark, consisting of the words "Bantam Books" and the
portrayal of a rooster, is Registered in U.S. Patent and
Trademark Office and in other countries. Marca Registrada.
Bantam Books, 666 Fifth Avenue, New York, New York 10103.

PRINTED IN THE UNITED STATES OF AMERICA

O   0 9 8 7 6 5 4 3 2 1

Prologue

He had loved Katherine Blue Song Gallatin for twenty-five years, and when he died tomorrow he would love her for eternity.

Justis Gallatin squinted both from the hot Arkansas sun and the blinding pain in his left arm, shattered by a Yankee bullet. His head aching with fatigue, briny sweat slipping through his mustache and into his mouth, he settled closer to the trunk of the aged pecan tree. The tree was his salvation and his tormentor; he was bound to it by six feet of thick iron chain which led to tight shackles around his booted ankles.

A shadow fell across Justis's face. He lifted his head wearily and met a sympathetic gaze. Justis smiled thinly. "A hot day in hell. Good work, Colonel."

"You ought to know."

The blue-coated colonel squatted by him, handed him a canteen, and accepted a nod as thanks. Justis filled his stomach with the cool liquid.

"Major Gallatin, if there's any message you want sent to your family, you best tell me today."

Justis slid his good hand inside the neck of his shirt and, ignoring the agony every movement sent through his body, lifted a chain with a gold nugget on it over his graying hair. He handed it to the officer.

"That came from my wife's land in Georgia." Justis shut his eyes for a moment, picturing the old Blue Song place, thinking of all it meant to Katie and all he'd done over the years to keep it for her.

He gazed intently into the colonel's eyes and said simply, "Tell her I'll be waiting there."

She had loved Justis Gallatin for twenty-five years, and she would love him for an eternity more. She would not let him step into that eternity alone and before his time.

Her pulse hammering with fear, Katherine entered the army tent and stood before the makeshift desk of a bearded, grim-faced Union officer. Colonel Nathaniel Chatham of the 1st Arkansas Cavalry stood and bowed slightly; he was obviously surprised as he took in her regal demeanor.

"I'd heard that you were beautiful and refined for a Cherokee woman," he said. "But the rumors don't do you enough credit, madam."

Katherine ignored the compliment. "You have no right to hold my husband prisoner here in Arkansas. He's a citizen of the Cherokee Nation."

"He's a white man. Living in the Oklahoma Injun lands doesn't change that."

"He's a citizen by marriage. He has sons who are half Cherokee. He served in the tribal government before the war." She paused, struggling to keep her dignity despite the growing terror for Justis's safety. "We're not part of your war, sir. Let him go."

Chatham stroked his graying-brown beard and gave her a hard look. "Madam, there's no use in trying to protect him or yourself. I know you were both born in Georgia. I know you've got Southern sentiments."

The colonel arched a brow. "And I know that your

husband is secretly an officer in the Confederate army. He and his Injuns spent the past two years bushwhacking Union troops all over Indian Territory."

"Because those troops didn't belong there."

"*No*. Because you Gallatins wanted to save your way of life. You owned fifty slaves. That showplace of yours over at Tahlequah was one of the biggest farms in the territory."

Katherine glared at him. "We've never owned slaves, Colonel. Those were freemen who worked for hire."

Looking stunned, Chatham studied her. Then he grimaced. "Doesn't matter. Major Gallatin is going to hang."

A rush of queasiness made lights dance in front of Katherine's eyes. She took a steadying breath. "Your troops have confiscated everything we owned. You ordered them to burn our house. My youngest son is in hiding because he shot a soldier who was trying to harm me. He's only thirteen years old, just a child. Haven't we suffered enough?"

"Madam, last month Injun soldiers killed my two eldest sons at the battle of Honey Springs." He paused. "And they scalped them."

Despair settled coldly in Katherine's chest. "My eldest sons fought for the Union," she told him. "One is dead and the other is in a Confederate prison."

"Your husband is a Reb and your sons enlisted for the Union side?" he asked, amazed.

"Yes. They went East and joined a regiment there so there'd be no chance of them fighting their own father one day." She paused, her throat aching. "It was an act of conscience and honor."

She and Chatham traded awkward, almost sympathetic looks. Katherine wondered if he had a kind-hearted soul beneath the bitterness war had brought him.

"Please, Colonel," she whispered. "I beg you to let my husband go."

He looked away wearily. "I'm a man of duty, madam. I can't turn a prisoner loose."

"Duty," she repeated with disdain. "You destroy my family and my home for duty." She raised one hand and pointed at the colonel, then murmured an incantation in Cherokee.

He glowered at her. "Madam, I've heard stories about your witchcraft. I'm not swayed by it."

"I'm a seer, not a *tsgili.* I cast no spells. I see what God intends. There will be a bond of darkness between my family and yours. Only God can change that."

She turned and glided from his tent, leaving him spellbound.

In his mind Justis relived his memories—the first time Katlanicha Blue Song, wary and full of fight, had shared his bed; the day she had admitted that she love him as much as he loved her; the marriage that had produced four fine children.

They had shared all the happiness that came from living *da-nitaka,* so close in spirit that they stood in each other's souls, and he loved her more now than he had the day they'd met.

"*Osiyo,* Father," a voice whispered behind him.

Justis turned slowly, all his senses alert. In the moonlight beyond the tree crouched a lanky boy dressed in buckskins, his black hair streaming down his back Indian style.

Pride and love mingled with fear in Justis. "Holt. Get out of here, Son. There's nothing you can do."

But Holt slipped soundlessly forward and fiddled with the manacles. With a sharp click they fell open. "Mother bribed a soldier to get the key."

Justis clasped his son's arm. "Your mother—"

"Is waiting for us." Holt's teeth flashed white in the darkness. "Put your good arm around my shoulder, Father, and let's leave this place behind."

• • •

She held Justis's head in her lap as Holt drove the wagon through the darkness. Crying silently, Katherine stroked a wet cloth across her husband's face.

He reached up and grasped her hand. "You weren't worried that those Yanks would hang an old buzzard like me, were you, Katie gal?" he whispered hoarsely.

"Sir, you gave me a fright." She bent over him, kissed him tenderly, and whispered, "How would I live without you?"

They were silent for a long moment, their lips not quite touching, his hand squeezing hers more tightly as he struggled for composure. Finally he asked, "Where'd you get enough money to bribe somebody for the key?"

"I traded the medallions to one of Chatham's men."

"Katie."

She shook her head. "Saving you was more important than saving some gold pieces from the old homeland. They were just a silly notion of mine, anyway." She slipped her hand inside his shirt, then gasped.

"I gave the nugget to Chatham," Justis told her. "He was supposed to send it to you after I was dead."

She stroked his chest. "Oh, husband. Then we have nothing left of the land but memories."

He drew her closer with his good hand. "The land will always be there waiting for us," he promised gently. "We'll go back."

Katherine rested her forehead on his and laid her hand over his heart, her fingers as light as a spirit.

Someday.

One

Nathan Chatham had lived in places so remote that even the *National Geographic* wouldn't visit them. He was an adopted member of primitive tribes in various regions of the world, including one in South America whose witch doctor had tattooed his right buttock while the whole village watched gleefully.

A few years later he'd added to his ornaments by getting the top of one ear pierced. The African chieftain had given him a choice—either have the ear pierced or have it cut off. Being a practical man, Nathan had chosen to get it pierced.

As a kid growing up just over the Arkansas border from the Cherokee Indian reservation, he'd assisted Cherokee shamans in ceremonies held for many purposes—from curing arthritis to conjuring up ghosts and talking wild birds down from their roosts.

Once as a very young man he'd shaved off his mustache and sprinkled the hair on a rose bed, just to see if it would really make the roses grow faster, as a shaman had said it would. The shaman had been right, much to Nathan's delight.

In short, Nathan had an abiding love and respect for other people's customs. But he'd never seen anything half so bizarre as this female wrestling match in the civilized environs of South Carolina.

The Beast Babe had just body-slammed Killerina to a limp pulp, and the crowd of mostly men was on its feet cheering. Nathan also stood, though his front-row seat made standing unnecessary. It just seemed polite.

A balding TV announcer in a tight blue suit climbed into the ring as the Beast Babe punched Killerina one more time, then stalked off toward the exit curtains. Killerina's attendants carried her away. Killerina managed a valiant wave good-bye.

"Ladies and gentlemen, I *hope* tonight's action doesn't get any more shocking than that!" the announcer bellowed into his microphone. "That was one of the nastiest battles I've ever seen on the Wild Women of Wrestling tour! Don't miss next week's revenge match between Killerina and the Beast Babe! That's next week, June seventeenth, at the fabulous Omni auditorium in Atlanta!"

Nathan smiled ruefully. Somehow he expected next week's match would be as nasty as this week's. "Nasty" made for sold-out tickets and TV time.

"And now for a duel of royal dimensions!" The announcer waved an arm toward the entrance aisle. Loudspeakers blared the well-known theme from a Wagnerian opera. The television cameras swiveled. "Ladies and gentlemen, get ready for . . . four hundred pounds of Lady Savage, the Valkyrie!"

A huge, mean-looking woman shoved the entrance curtains aside and came marching down the aisle, giant metal cones thrust forward on her chest, a horned helmet perched atop her short, punk-cut blonde hair. She wore gold wrestling boots, white tights, and a short white skirt cinched with a wide belt covered in rhinestones. Everything on her and around her jiggled.

"I vill de-STROY mein opponent!" Lady Savage screeched in a bad German accent. The crowd booed lustily and yelled rude things as Lady Savage hoisted herself into the ring. She went around the perimeter shaking a long spear.

Nathan sat down and tried not to laugh his tattoo off. He couldn't wait to see what Kat Gallatin looked like.

The announcer said in solemn tones, "Only one woman in professional wrestling has the talent, the heart, and the sheer *raw courage* to face Lady Savage!"

The loudspeakers sent hokey tom-tom music reverberating through the room. "Fans, put your hands together for that fabulous Indian, that pride of the Cherokee people, the incredible Princess Talana!"

Nathan's laughter faded. What the hell? She used some sort of Indian persona? He stood up and trained his gaze on the curtains at the back of the small auditorium.

Kat Gallatin, alias Princess Talana, bounded through the curtains and scampered up the aisle with the lithe, graceful stride of a gymnast. A colorful warbonnet covered her head and fluttered all the way to her moccasined heels. Her face was streaked with gaudy war paint.

Nathan simply stared at her. She couldn't have been much more than five feet tall, with a lovely little face despite the goo, and a body that was curvaceous and slender. Every curve knew its place, he thought. Man, did it know.

All she wore was a buckskin miniskirt and a fringed buckskin halter top. Her skin was a beautiful honey color and she'd oiled her legs so that their movements produced a symphony of delicate, gleaming muscle.

She leapt to the edge of the ring and perched there holding the top rope, one arm raised to salute the crowd. Cheers rocked the ceiling when she blew kisses and gave everyone a dazzling smile which crinkled her deep-set eyes impishly.

"Me heap happy to see you! How!" she yelled, and held up one hand, palm forward in a gesture no Indian outside a bad B-rated Western had ever used.

"I know how, just give me a chance!" someone shouted.

Nathan felt grim disgust settle in his stomach. What kind of woman would willingly make a mockery out of her heritage for the entertainment of a bunch of drooling rednecks?

Five generations of Chathams had lived close to the Cherokees, starting when great-great-grandfather Nathaniel settled his family near Indian Territory before the Civil War. The Chathams had a lot of grudges against the Gallatins, but they'd always respected the Cherokee culture.

Obviously, Kat Gallatin did not.

Men and boys were going berserk around Nathan, stomping their feet, shouting her name, calling out blue remarks.

"Whip the Valkyrie's butt, squaw!"

"Tickle me with those feathers!"

"Let me be an Injun lover!"

"Take me to your wigwam, baby, oh, take me to your wigwam!"

This joke of hers wasn't funny at all.

Nathan hadn't expected Kat Gallatin to use her Indian heritage like a bawdy gimmick. He hadn't counted on her being so lovely and graceful that he wanted to haul her away from these damned gawking men and warn her about the snickering comments they made in low voices that she couldn't hear.

She climbed into the ring, took her warbonnet off, and shook free two black braids that fell all the way to her hips. Then she grinned and gave the crowd a cheerful thumbs-up. She managed to look adorable and mischievous rather than tacky.

Nathan sat down, frowning. He hadn't counted on feeling this guilt either. He'd just wanted to see one of the Gallatin cousins up close before he took revenge on them and their land.

Someone had once told Kat that wrestling was really a simple morality play—good versus evil, right versus wrong. Having gotten no more than a very basic high school education from tutors hired by the circus, Kat wasn't too sure what a morality play was.

But she knew that Lady Savage was definitely evil, wrong, and just plain ticked off.

"Jeez, Muffie, calm down. You're the winner tonight," Kat choked out at a private moment while Lady Savage had her down on the mat in a pretzellike contortion. "I know you've had a bad day, but don't try to kill me."

"Sorry," Muffie grunted. "I hate men and this is a good outlet for my aggression."

She let Kat thump her in the neck and fell backward, flailing her beefy arms dramatically. Kat staggered to her feet, feeling so pummeled that she didn't have to fake it as she usually did.

Rent. Car payment. Those were her silent mantras as she wavered to the ropes and slumped over them. This was a heck of a way to make a living, but the money was decent.

The crowd yelled at her to watch out, that Lady Savage was coming up behind her. Kat took a reviving breath. Okay, so she'd struggle pathetically to get off the ropes, then turn around and kick Muffie in the stomach, just like in rehearsal.

"Arrrrgh! Svine! Indian svine!" Muffie clamped a hand to the back of Kat's neck, then wound the other hand into her leather skirt. Kat grimaced with discomfort as Muffie jerked her off the ropes. The leather skirt had built-in leather panties.

Lord, she hated getting a wedgie.

But the men in the audience loved it, of course, because they paid to see good bodies as well as good body slams. Kat had spent most of her life wearing revealing costumes of some kind or other, so like any other professional athlete, she barely noticed the ogling.

She just wished she knew what Muffie had in mind next.

Muffie hoisted her overhead and walked around the ring, snarling. Kat tightened her torso so that her back wouldn't get hurt, then hung there looking desperate and trapped.

"This is awful!" the announcer screamed. "Audience, please, please, don't provoke Lady Savage! You never know what she's going to do when she gets in this mood!"

Kat bit her lip to keep from smiling as the audience immediately began to chant insults at Muffie. This was a very effective change in the routine.

But then Muffie bellowed, "Men!" and launched Kat at the front row.

There was no warning and no time to coordinate her fall. She broadsided a hard masculine chest and bounced her forehead off the victim's chin. His folding chair skidded backward and collapsed, dumping both him and her on the auditorium's concrete floor.

Wincing from the pain in her forehead, Kat was only dimly aware of his grunt of discomfort as she sank an elbow into the man's thigh. He grabbed her hands, pulled them around his neck, and slid his arms under her.

"This means he gets to keep her!" someone shouted.

Kat heard other, more bawdy observations on the victim's luck, and she began to get embarrassed.

"Sorry, man, sorry," she whispered between gasps for breath. "The routine doesn't usually get this crazy."

"I want combat pay."

The deep, slightly drawling voice made her tilt her head back and look at him. And the sight of him was more of a jolt than having been tossed by Muffie.

Gunmetal-gray eyes looked back at her with an intensity that belied the lazy, sensual droop of the lids. They were part of a weathered face with a handsomely battered nose and a dark brown mustache over a wide, strong mouth.

His face looked as if it had visited a lot of places where life was interesting but not easy. His nose looked as though the visits hadn't always been welcome.

His chocolate-colored hair was neat but rakishly long, and he wore a gold stud in the top of his left ear. *Ouch.* He had either been very stupid or very macho when he had got his ear pierced right in the thickest part of the cartilage.

Danger, girl, danger, she thought.

"Just let go of me," she whispered.

"You look like you're in pain."

I always look this way when I'm hypnotized.

"It's part of the act," she said softly.

"Oh." His eyes narrowed in dismay and he loosened his grip. "You have to let go of me, too."

Kat realized that she'd wound her hands into his V-necked sweater. Its soft blue material had an expensive feel to it, as if it might be cashmere, and she had twisted it into wads.

"Sorry, dude."

With that blithe reply she let go and rolled away from him. Once she was out of his startling embrace, she connected with the world again and realized that the crowd was in a frenzy and Muffie was headed straight for her.

Muffie had a wild look in her eyes.

"Oh Lord," Kat said plaintively.

She decided to act terrified—since that wouldn't take much effort at the moment—and covered her head with her arms. Peeking out, Kat saw Muffie grab a folding chair and raised it menacingly.

Oh no. If Muffie didn't do the chair bit just right, it would be curtains—hospital curtains—for Princess Talana. Muffie didn't look too interested in technique at the moment.

"She's not pretending," Mr. Pierced Ear observed grimly.

"You got that right," Kat told him. She leapt to her feet. One of the cardinal rules of wrestling was to keep the mayhem out of the audience. Promoters didn't like lawsuits from injured fans.

"Just stay on the floor," Kat ordered. "I'll head her off."

But this fan didn't want protection. In a flash he was on his feet, too, pushing her aside with an outstretched arm. Kat bumped into the arm and stopped, gazing at him in shock as he stepped in front of her.

He wasn't overly tall or overly big, but there was a powerful, long-legged body inside that cashmere sweater, those faded jeans and—how odd, she thought —those leather moccasins.

And Muffie was going to kill him.

Kat grabbed his shoulder. "Her sister ran off with her boyfriend today," she hissed into the stranger's unpierced ear. "She hates men right now. Get out of her way."

Instead he held up both hands to Muffie in a placating gesture. Muffie raised the chair higher and advanced like a runaway bulldozer. The announcer was calling for the security guards. The audience was calling for blood.

"Put the chair down," that deep, resonant voice told Muffie calmly.

"I'll put it down your throat if you don't move!" she retorted.

She swung the chair and he caught one leg of it with a deft twisting motion of his hand. Muffie lost her hold and the chair fell to the floor.

She balled her fists and took a swing at him. He stepped back and the punch missed him by a bare inch. Kat felt the wind of it on her face.

Kat groaned inwardly. Pierced Ear was a gentleman. He wouldn't fight back. She admired that, but she couldn't let him get stomped because of it.

She ducked around him and charged Muffie, who kicked her in the ankle. Kat gasped as a pain like hot needles stabbed through her leg. She didn't have much time to wonder what the snapping sensation meant, though, because she had to save this fascinating man who wouldn't save himself.

Raising one fist, she cuffed Muffie on the jaw. Muffie pressed both hands to her face and staggered back, looking pitifully shocked. Kat ran up to her and said sadly, "I had to do it, kid. You can't trash members of the audience."

"You hit me on my abscessed tooth!"

"I know. I'll do it again if you don't behave."

By then the security guards and a bunch of the other wrestlers were on the scene. They grabbed Muffie and tugged her toward the exit amidst frenzied booing.

Kat's pulse felt thready and a sick prickling sensation ran over her shoulders. Her ankle was on fire.

The stranger grabbed her elbow. "You're limping." His voice held concern, but then he added sarcastically, "Or is it just part of this stupid routine?"

Kat turned to look at the rebuking expression on his face, and her admiration was replaced by dull fury.

She knew that look, that aura of disgust from men who thought she was a low-rent joke, maybe not much different from women who mud-wrestled naked in a strip joint.

"It's part of the routine," she told him, and pulled her arm away. "Thanks for playing along."

"The routine stinks."

"Hey, sweetcakes, when I want a lecture, I'll go to college."

"Do that. Get a real job. And stop selling yourself as a Cherokee. It's an insult."

Her stomach churned queasily from embarrassment and pain. What did he know about the way she'd grown up? Nothing! Who was he to act arrogant? "I should have let Muf—Lady Savage beat your brains out," Kat replied. "It would have been a small job."

She whipped around and hobbled toward the exit, blushing with humiliation and anger. Thanks to her skin tone, she knew Pierced Ear hadn't noticed the blush.

Agonizing jolts shot up her leg as she tried not to limp on it. *He* was responsible for this. If he hadn't tried to be a nice guy when he really didn't want to be . . .

The audience was cheering wildly. People reached out to slap her on the back and tug playfully at her braided hair. One of the other wrestlers, Maniac Mary, trotted up and put a supportive arm under her shoulders.

"Lean on me, Kat. Think something's broken?" she whispered.

"Yes."

"Don't be so tough. Stop trying to walk on it or you'll make it worse. Go for the sympathy shtick."

Kat sighed with defeat and leaned heavily against her friend. She blew kisses to the audience and wanted to cry because she knew what the stranger thought of her now.

Jeez, Kat thought, there was everything here on the reservation but Indians.

She lifted her left foot from the gas pedal—she had her injured foot propped up on the dashboard—and let her Mustang creep along in bumper-to-bumper tourist traffic. On either side of the wide street were shops advertising Cherokee crafts and souvenirs, but with names such as Powwow Paul's she doubted that the merchandise was authentic.

In the distance the rounded, blue-green North Carolina mountains towered over the tourist district like a reminder that once this had been unbroken wilderness inhabited only by Cherokees.

There was a reservation here in North Carolina and another one in Oklahoma. It was confusing. From what little she'd read so far Kat understood that a few hundred refugees had hidden here in these rugged mountains when the tribe was forced to leave the South.

There was an Indian! Kat parked her car in a space in front of a shop, grabbed her crutch and the oversized tote bag that served as her purse, then hobbled over to the tall, majestic-looking old man in buckskins and a warbonnet. A woven basket sat at his feet.

"Hi ya," she said cheerfully. "Are you a chief?"

He looked her up and down, taking in everything from her pink Reeboks to her jeans, the T-shirt that read *WOW—Wild Women of Wrestling*, and finally, her face and hair. His lips twitched with amusement.

"*Osiyo, wah lay lee.*"

Kat smiled at him, transfixed. "Is that Cherokee?"

He nodded.

"What did you say?"

"Hello, hummingbird." He tilted his head and looked at her curiously. "You aren't from around here."

"Nah. But I'm a Cherokee. I just don't know anything about the tribe—yet. I came up here to see my cousin."

He held out a gnarled hand. "My name's Sam Tall Wolf."

They shook. "I'm Kat Gallatin."

His eyes widened. "You are Eh-lee-ga's cousin?"

"Eh-lee-ga?"

"Erica. Erica Gallatin."

"Yeah! I just met her a month ago. We inherited some land together, us and our cousin Tess from

California. The land's in Georgia, but the lady who owned it lived up here."

Sam Tall Wolf nodded solemnly. "Dove Gallatin. She was a friend of mine from way back."

"That's great! How can I find her place? Erica came down here from Washington to research the family. She's moved into Dove's house for a while."

"I know." Sam thumped his chest. "My grandson's in love with her."

Shocked, Kat tried not to totter on her crutch. Only four weeks ago she'd gone to Georgia to meet with Erica and Tess Gallatin for the first time, but they'd become close quickly. Erica had definitely been unattached four weeks ago. In fact, she'd called herself the last old maid in Washington, D.C.

Obviously, Erica had found a lot more than Gallatin family history down here.

"Uh. Mr. Tall Wolf—"

"Call me Grandpa Sam. All the Real People do."

"Uh, Real People?"

"Cherokees. The *Ani-Yun-Wiya*."

Kat wanted to laugh with delight. She was not only a hummingbird, she was a Real Person. "Can you tell me how to find Dove's house?"

"Sure." He gave her directions.

"Grandpa Sam, what exactly are you doing here?" She pointed to the basket.

"Chiefing. People want their pictures made with a real Cherokee. They take a picture, I get a tip." He gestured toward the warbonnet. "Course, our people never wore stuff like this, but the tourists expect it."

Kat looked at him sheepishly, thinking of the stranger's insult a couple of nights ago. "Do you ever feel funny about dressing up this way to make money? I mean, I wrestle for a living, and—"

"Now I remember. Princess Talana!" He snapped his fingers. "I've seen you on TV! You're great!"

She wanted to hug him. "Do you think I'm making fun of being an Indian? Is it bad?"

He chucked her under the chin. "You do what you got to do, *wah lay lee.* Inside, here"—he pointed to his heart—"this is the only place you worry about. If you're a Cherokee here, you're okay."

"Grandpa Sam, I don't have much family. Can I adopt you?"

"Sure."

He was still grinning when she drove away.

Erica Gallatin came from a branch of the family that had not married back into the tribe. As a result, she was a lanky, tall redhead with skin like a lily. The only physical resemblance she and Kat shared were green eyes, which apparently had been passed along from their great-great-grandfather Justis. Erica was educated and proper, with a little bit of a Yankee accent, but she was no snob. Kat admired her tremendously.

They sat in Dove Gallatin's cute little frame house in the midst of the woods, chatting as if they'd known each other forever.

"Have you got your medallion?" Erica asked.

"Oh yeah. I've been wearing it." She pulled a chain from under the neck of her T-shirt. The heavy gold piece swung from it gently, catching the afternoon light. It was stamped with mysterious Cherokee writing on both sides.

"Grandpa Sam will translate it for you, if you want to leave it. He's already working on mine and Tess's."

"Great!" Kat handed her the gold piece. "Maybe we'll figure out what in the world ol' Dove wanted us to know."

Erica looked at Kat's taped ankle anxiously. "You're sure that you don't need any money? A loan? Don't be shy. We're family."

"Nah. I'm gonna camp out on our land in Gold Ridge while my ankle heals, and that won't cost much. I'm used to living simple." She winked at

Erica and wished her confidence were as great as she made it sound. "Us Injuns don't need much but our dignity, you know."

And after the other night, she wasn't certain she even had that.

It was one of the most beautiful places she'd ever seen, this hilly forested land with its wide valley and lazy, gurgling stream. And the amazing thing was, it was part hers.

Hers. Kat Gallatin—the nomad, a woman who'd spent a great part of her twenty-eight years on the road or in cheap apartments, now owned a one-third interest in two hundred acres in Gold Ridge, Georgia. She felt very important.

She limped along a trail through wild honeysuckle and rhododendron, using her crutch to push low-hanging dogwood branches aside. At the edge of the stream she stopped and inhaled the cool, earthy scent.

Her great-great-grandmother Katlanicha Blue Song had been born on this land, and she'd made certain that it would stay in the family forever. The medallions had something to do with that, but they were still a big mystery to her and her cousins.

Lord, it was so secluded here, the June day was sticky, and her ankle throbbed from too much walking. Kat eyed the stream for a moment, then sat down and removed everything but her bra and panties. She took the elastic tape off her ankle and waded into the stream.

Kat sat down in a shallow part and leaned back on her elbows so that the water rushed over her lower body. Finally she lay down completely, with just her face protruding from the icy water and her hair floating around her like a black cloud.

It felt so right to be here; she felt so close to something, to *someone* she'd never known, that her chest constricted with happiness and homesickness and the odd notion that she'd lain here like this before.

Hah. *Déjà vu.* A chemical quirk in the brain. She'd heard it explained on a talk show once. There were no surprises in the modern world.

Kat sighed, stretched, then reached behind her and unhooked her bra. She wound it into a ball and shot it to the grassy bank with an expert overhand pitch.

It hit Pierced Ear right in the face.

Two

This was what it felt like to burn up from the inside out, to die from embarrassment. She wanted to dissolve into the water and float away.

He knelt on one knee, wearing nothing but khaki shorts and jogging shoes, his arm propped nonchalantly on his updrawn leg, her bra dangling coyly from his brawny hand. He looked like the kind of man who was used to having women throw their underwear at him.

Even though her breasts were underwater, Kat draped an arm across them. He tracked her actions with a rueful gaze. She stared at him speechlessly.

"Hello again," he said without smiling, although there was a hint of victorious humor in his gray eyes.

Finally her brain cleared. Had this man been following her since the other night? Had he followed her all the way from South Carolina? What did he want? Had he protected her before with the intention of harming her in some way now?

"I have friends with me," she lied through clenched teeth. "They're at the end of the old trail, with my car, but they'll be here any minute."

He gave her a rebuking look. "No they won't. I watched you unload your car. You're alone."

Dread filled her stomach. "Why are you following me? What do you want?"

He tossed her bra onto a holly bush, then sat down and crossed his legs. His chest and arms were darkly tanned. Even at a distance she could see sun-lightened brown hair on his chest and patches of freckles on his shoulders.

"Relax, Princess Talana. I'm not here to body-slam you."

He idly stroked a gold nugget that hung from a slender gold chain around his neck. The nugget nestled seductively in a patch of brown-blond hair at the center of his chest. Ropy muscles flexed around it when he shifted his position.

"Why'd you follow me?" she demanded again.

Kat would have bet money that this man hadn't gotten his physique or his tan at a health club, and that the gold nugget hadn't come from a jewelry store. Considering his attitude, the longish hair, and the pierced ear, he was probably a Hell's Angel looking for a girlfriend.

"I'm not following you," he assured her. "I was here first." He pointed over his right shoulder. "I have a camp in the bend of the stream back that way."

"This is private property. Did you know that?"

"Yep."

"In fact, this is my property."

"Yep. I know."

"How do you know?"

"You're Kat Gallatin. You have two distantly related cousins. The three of you just inherited this land from a nearly full-blooded Cherokee woman named Dove Gallatin, up in North Carolina. This land has been in the Gallatin family for at least a hundred and fifty years—probably a lot longer than that, since it belonged to your great-great-grandmother's people, and they were Cherokees of the blue clan."

Kat gaped at him. She couldn't help it. He knew almost as much about her family history as she did. "Who *are* you?"

"Does the name Chatham mean anything to you?"

She shook her head. "Should it?"

He stared at her hard for several seconds. "I'm with Tri-State Mining."

"Oh. Oh!" Still, she frowned at him in bewilderment. "What are you doing here? We haven't signed any agreement to lease the mining rights."

"Not yet, anyway."

"I don't think we're going to, either. At least not until we learn more about our different branches of the family."

"Hmmm. Well, I'm just a geologist. Doing some studies for the company. Harmless stuff. Soil samples, nothing to worry about."

Kat looked down at the icy water rushing over her body. She was beginning to shiver, both from the water and his provocative stare. The man was used to looking at naked women through those droopy bedroom eyes of his. He didn't seem the least bit eager to stop enjoying her situation.

"This is ridiculous. I'd like to get out of the water."

"Go ahead. I didn't think you were the modest type."

"I'm not the immodest type, either," she said grimly. "Look, you're confirming my suspicion that you're a stuck-up jerk. And a dirty-minded jerk, too. And whatever your name is, Chat-ham, I want you off this land."

"Nope. You'll need your cousins' agreement to kick me off, and I heard that your cousin Tess is out of the country."

"Jeez, you're a regular fountain of information about us Gallatins. Did Tri-State have us investigated?"

"Yep. I know that you and your cousins were all born on the same day, different years. Very interesting. Some people might say it means something. You're twenty-eight, Erica's thirty-three, and Tess's twenty-six. Erica lives in Washington, D.C. Tess lives in Long Beach, California."

He smiled wickedly, enjoying himself. "They've got money; you don't. You drive an old Mustang which you bought used five years ago, and you have a cheap apartment in Miami. If you're late with next month's rent, you're going to be evicted. I'd say you need the deal Tri-State's offering."

Kat shook with anger. She felt invaded, violated, and more naked than ever. How dare a man who owned cashmere sweaters and wore a gold nugget poke fun at her poverty!

"Get the hell away from me."

He stood up. "The name's Nathan Chatham. Geologist. In the mining business I'm called a gunslinger."

"In my business you're called a pain in the backside."

"Speaking of pain," he said sweetly, "you're a great actress. That limp was perfect the other night. Pitiful. You really looked pitiful. The injured Indian maiden. What a hoot."

Her eyes burned. "Don't be surprised if I *don't* visit your camp."

"So what are you doing here? Studying nature?" He drew himself up and looked around solemnly, as if imitating her. "Hmmm. Heap pretty. Trees. Water. Where fast-food restaurant?"

She understood why her people had once gone around scalping white men. It must have been great fun.

"I'm camping here, too," she told him.

That brought the first honest look of surprise to his face. "You're camping? Can't afford a motel?"

That's right, wise guy, she told him silently. "I was born in a circus tent, sweetcakes. I've spent most of my life on the road. I can outcamp you any day."

He laughed richly. "I doubt it. Where are you setting up?"

Kat thought if she didn't get out of the water soon her smaller body parts would freeze and fall off. Fingers, toes, nipples—the only thing saving them now was the heat generated by anger at Nathan Chatham.

She tilted her head and smiled widely, without any trace of sincerity. "Naaah, I don't want you to tell the cavalry where to find me after I loot and pillage you."

"It's *ravish*, loot, and pillage. Don't forget that part of the attack. I'll be disappointed if you don't ravish me."

Smiling, he strode off through the woods—*her* woods, dammit—as if he owned them.

Nathan sat in front of his tipi brooding about Kat Gallatin. He couldn't help being fascinated with her, and that made him uncomfortable. The last thing he wanted was to go soft on his plans for this acreage, and it was difficult enough to keep his goal focused now that he'd seen the land.

It was undeniably special, with its wide green valley and picturesque hillsides. From the high ridge overlooking the valley he could see blue-green mountains in the distance, the southern foothills of the Smokies, Place of the Blue Smoke, as the Cherokees had called them.

There were good-sized trout in the stream, the woods were full of wildlife—besides Kat Gallatin, who was at least exotic, if not wild—and the air had a sweet clean scent which made him feel fresh inside.

On the other hand Kat Gallatin made him feel hot inside, a little bit like a roll with too much yeast baking. Everything rose high and fast.

Lord, the woman was accustomed to provoking men with her athletic little bundle of curves, and she'd lain there in that stream like a seductive Cherokee water nymph, letting that beautiful black mane of hair swirl around her as if she knew he couldn't help admiring it.

She'd returned his jaunty inspection without batting an eyelash, and he'd felt a reckless urge to walk out in the stream just to see what she'd do—and what he'd do when she did it.

Dammit, this was probably how Dove Gallatin had seduced and ruined his weak-willed grandpa.

Nathan filled a long pipe with tobacco, lit it, and took a few calming puffs as he set up the fire for dinner. He wouldn't use his camp stove tonight; he'd wrap some fresh-caught trout in leaves and mud, then bake them.

And after dark he'd pay a neighborly visit to Kat Gallatin. This was probably the first time a Cherokee had spent the night on this land in a century and a half. He hoped she would appreciate it while she could.

Here she was trying to camp out as her ancestors had done, and her ancestors hadn't camped out at all.

Kat pulled a plaid stadium blanket farther around her shoulders and hunched over the Cherokee history book Erica had loaned her. She'd hung several kerosene lanterns from a rope strung between two walnut trees, and in the flickering light she read how the tribe had become "civilized" by about 1800.

They'd kept a lot of their native culture, but many of them had adopted some white ways, too, including farming, business, formal education—and living in houses! She wanted a house *immediately* so she'd be authentic.

Smiling to herself, Kat poked at her campfire, stuck another hot dog on the end of a coat hanger, and balanced it against a log at the edge of the flames. In her life she'd eaten enough campfire hot dogs to choke a Girl Scout. Tomorrow she'd get organized and break out some canned soup.

Tomorrow she'd probably have to confront Nathan Chatham again. As usual, her thoughts strayed back to him. She'd driven ten miles to Gold Ridge that afternoon to check him out with T. Lucas Brown, the lawyer who'd handled Dove's will. Yes, Chatham was with Tri-State Mining, and he had let Brown know that he was exploring the Gallatin land.

Brown hadn't seen any harm in it. There wouldn't be any harm, Kat agreed silently, if Chatham weren't such a wise guy. An arrogant, ruggedly appealing wise guy with the kind of knowing eyes that told her he'd been to a lot of exciting places and done a lot of exciting things—some of them undoubtedly between the sheets.

Kat shook her head. Better go back to reading before she thought much along that line. She'd been lonely too long to entertain images of Nathan Chatham wearing nothing but his gold.

Something big growled in the bushes beyond her tent. Kat's head snapped up, and goose bumps rose on her skin. A bear? Nah, this part of north Georgia was a little too developed for bears to survive. A bobcat? An extra from a horror movie? A frog with an adenoid problem?

It growled again. All right, what would great-great-grandmother Katherine, for whom she was named, have done now?

Kat pulled a 9mm Beretta automatic from under her blanket, pointed it at a patch of starlight between the tree branches, and blasted six warning shots into the night sky.

"You got me," a deep voice said, then groaned. Kat twisted frantically to watch Nathan Chatham stumble out of the bushes, clutching his chest with all the hokey drama of a bad actor. "Right through the heart." He sank to the ground, rolled over on his back, and flopped both arms out.

Stunned, she stared at him openmouthed. Laughter was her first inclination, but the man had tried to scare her, and that was too annoying.

The fact that he wore nothing but low-slung leather breeches and moccasins didn't help her warring emotions. He lay there, his hairy chest rising and falling swiftly, his belly showing off a washboard of muscles, his soft leather pants clinging all too intimately to the masculine bulge between his thighs.

Kat's pulse skittered. What was he, some sort of a back-to-nature type? Daniel Boone with an earring?

She snatched her coat hanger with the hot dog on it from its perch over the fire and smacked him across the stomach. He yelped as hot dog and hot wire hit the skin just below his navel.

Kat thought it surprising that he didn't say one obscene word as he flung himself upright, holding his stomach with one hand. *A gentleman*, she wondered, as she had when he had refused to defend himself against Muffie.

Nah. He was just too shocked to cuss. His eyes looked like cold pewter as he frowned at her. Underneath the dark mustache his mouth pressed into a thin line of warning. Then it pursed with failing control, and one corner crooked up.

"You little hellion," he said gruffly. "But I deserved that."

Inside she sighed with relief. "I know you did." They both sniffed at a pungent burning odor. Kat bit her lower lip to keep from smiling. She'd singed his stomach hair.

"I'm singed," he said, his eyes never leaving hers. "My pelt's worthless now."

"It was worthless before."

He removed his hand and looked down at himself. Kat, who still held the Beretta in one hand and the coat hanger with its lethal hot dog in the other, followed his gaze and grimaced at the thin red streak just above his breeches.

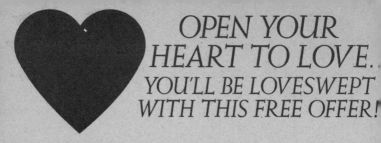

OPEN YOUR HEART TO LOVE..
YOU'LL BE LOVESWEPT WITH THIS FREE OFFER!

HERE'S WHAT YOU GET:

1. FREE! SIX NEW LOVESWEPT NOVELS! You get 6 beautiful stories filled with passion, romance, laughter, and tears...exciting romances to stir the excitement of falling in love... again and again.

2. FREE! A BEAUTIFUL MAKEUP CASE WITH A MIRROR THAT LIGHTS UP! What could be more useful than a makeup case with a mirror that lights up*? Once you open the tortoise-shell finish case, you have a choice of brushes...for your lips, your eyes, and your blushing cheeks.

*(batteries not included)

3. SAVE! MONEY-SAVING HOME DELIVERY! Join the Loveswept at-home reader service and we'll send you 6 new novels each month. You always get 15 days to preview them before you decide. Each book is yours for only $2.09 — a savings of 41¢ per book.

4. BEAT THE CROWDS! You'll always receive your Loveswept books before they are available in bookstores. You'll be the first to thrill to these exciting new stories.

BE LOVESWEPT TODAY — JUST COMPLETE, DETACH AND MAIL YOUR FREE-OFFER CARD.

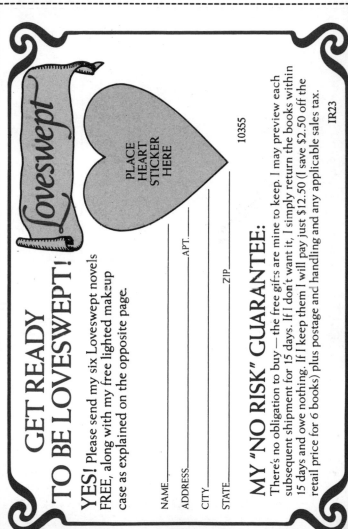

FREE–LIGHTED MAKEUP CASE!
FREE–6 LOVESWEPT NOVELS!

- NO OBLIGATION
- NO PURCHASE NECESSARY

GET READY TO BE LOVESWEPT!

YES! Please send my six Loveswept novels FREE, along with my free lighted makeup case as explained on the opposite page.

Loveswept

PLACE HEART STICKER HERE

NAME _____

ADDRESS _____ APT. _____

CITY _____

STATE _____ ZIP _____

10355

MY "NO RISK" GUARANTEE:

There's no obligation to buy — the free gifts are mine to keep. I may preview each subsequent shipment for 15 days. If I don't want it, I simply return the books within 15 days and owe nothing. If I keep them I will pay just $12.50 (I save $2.50 off the retail price for 6 books) plus postage and handling and any applicable sales tax.

IR23

(DETACH AND MAIL CARD TODAY.)

REMEMBER!

- The free books and gift are mine to keep!
- There is no obligation!
- I may preview each shipment for 15 days!
- I can cancel anytime!

"I have some burn ointment," she offered.

"Don't need it." He took the hot dog, ate half of it, then rubbed the other half on his stomach.

"Pretty disgusting."

"Thank you."

"What are you doing in my camp, besides using my food in weird ways?"

He leaned back on his elbows, and the firelight gleamed on the gold nugget against his chest. "I came to see how real Indians live."

Looking around, he nodded his approval at her simple canvas tent and basic camping gear, at the way she'd scraped leaves back from the dark, loamy soil so her campfire wouldn't spread, and at the sack of groceries stowed safely away from animals in a nylon net tied to a tree limb. "Not bad."

"I told you before, I know how to camp." She tucked the Beretta out of sight under her blanket.

"And how to defend yourself?"

"Yeah."

"Real bullets or fake ones?" he asked, and gave her a slit-eyed smile of challenge.

Kat arched her brow at him. "Hide in the bushes again and take your chances."

"Ouch." He reached over and took the book from her lap. "Hmmm. I didn't know wrestlers could read."

That remark stung badly. Her eyes smarting with tears of anger, she snatched the book back from him. "I'm not a genius, but I'm not dumb. Go back to your own side of the woods."

He winced a little. "Look, I didn't mean—"

"Go on, college boy."

"College boy?" He gave her a droll look. "Nobody's called me 'boy' since I hit thirty . . . and that was five years ago. Now why do I suspect that you don't think much of a college education?"

"I think a lot of it. Someday I'm gonna get one. I just don't like college jerks who look down at people who don't have a little piece of paper with their name on it."

"I never graduated from college. I only went for about a year."

"But you're a geologist."

"Who said you need to go to college to learn what you want to know?"

Kat looked away and fiddled with the cover of her book for a moment. "My husband said so."

There was suddenly an alertness, a subtle tightening of Nathan Chatham's body and an intensity in his eyes that made her look at him askance. "You surprised that somebody like me would have been married once? Women wrestlers are real women, ya know."

He smiled carefully, and the intensity faded as if he'd willed it away. "So you're not hitched anymore?"

She glanced away, clenching her teeth. "Right."

"I'm not judging you. Quit looking defensive."

Kat snapped her gaze back to him. "All you do is judge me. Starting with the other night."

"Well, men tend to get ideas about half-naked women who land in their laps. Look, Kitty Kat, wrestling is just sex and violence pretending to be a sport. That goes for men's wrestling as well as women's. Don't tell me you're surprised when people treat you like a hot babe."

"Oh, I get it. You snuck over to my camp tonight because you think I'm easy. You look down your nose at me but you wouldn't mind slumming to get a little nighttime entertainment."

The tension simmered in him again, more than ever. He lifted a hand slowly, pointed one blunt-tipped finger at her, and said in a soft, deadly voice, "That accusation says a lot more about your opinion of yourself than my opinion of you."

"I have a good opinion of myself. It's just that I have to go around defending it with guys like you."

"Guys like me? You mean guys you dislike before you know a damn thing about them?"

"So tell me something to change my mind."

He squinted thoughtfully. Then he lifted the nugget from his chest. "I look for gold. Even when I see nothing but dirt, I can tell that there's something precious underneath. And I treasure it."

Kat straightened ominously. "You calling me dirt?"

He groaned, laughed wearily, and fell back on the leafy soil. "No. I'm calling you trouble. Trouble on the surface, trouble underneath."

"Gee, thanks," she said dryly. "I'll just consider the source. You're a strange man. Like you don't fit in with the rest of the world."

"Good. Don't want to."

"Me either."

They traded a long look that sent primal sensations up Kat's spine, making her feel achy and relaxed inside. She looked back at her book, a little desperate to escape the magnetic pull of his gaze. "I've got reading to do. I'm trying to learn about Cherokees." She smiled tentatively. "My nickname is *Wis-sah* in Cherokee. Cat."

He nodded as if he knew that, being polite, she guessed.

She watched him get to his feet, moving with the easy, slow confidence that seemed to characterize everything he did. She could smell him, smell the leather, the pleasant musk of his sweat, and a fragrant scent that reminded her of rich earth after a rain.

"You smoke?" she asked.

"Smoke a pipe sometimes." He smiled at her quizzical expression. "Nothing funny. Just tobacco. Does the smell bother you?"

"Cigarettes do. But pipes and cigars don't." She tilted her head to one side and studied him raptly. A Hell's Angel type wouldn't smoke a pipe—not with tobacco in it, at any rate. But it didn't jibe. When she thought of pipes, she pictured Fred MacMurray, not a wild man like Nathan who ran around dressed like a frontier gypsy.

"How long are you going to camp out here?" she asked.

"Don't know. There's no hurry. How about you?"

Kat thought of her fractured ankle, hidden under the blanket. "Three or four weeks, maybe."

"Whew! Here by yourself? Don't you have any family? No tomcat wondering where you went?"

"Nope. Well, no family other than the cousins I met a while back, Erica and Tess. We've kind of got this bond, see? 'Cause of being the only Gallatins left and being born on the same day."

He studied her silently, obviously puzzling over her mysteries. Well, let him puzzle. The last thing a nomad like her needed was to get too chatty with a man who looked at her the way Nathan Chatham did: with a man-woman invitation in his eyes.

She suspected that it might be hard to leave this man behind. For sheer fascination, he was unique. Even worse, what if it was like her marriage, and he did the leaving? Good grief, she'd just met him, and she was already mad at him for deserting her.

"I love it here," she told Nathan. "I want to soak up the vibes and get into the family history. I think I'm gonna come back here someday and build a little house. Yeah."

She nodded firmly but wondered where that notion had come from. Until this moment she hadn't thought about settling on this land, but suddenly it was the only natural thing to do, as if she'd known all along that she was going to live here eventually.

Kat forgot her odd musings when she saw the troubled, almost angry expression on Nathan Chatham's face.

"Aw, a woman like you wouldn't be happy here," he said in an offhand way. "There's nothing to do but stare at the trees."

Kat huffed at him. Just when she thought he was okay, he turned grumpy again. "So what would a 'woman like me' be happy doing?"

"Show biz. You were in your element the other night."

"What you're saying is that I'm flamboyant and I probably couldn't lead a normal life, huh?"

"Right."

Lord, did he know *exactly* which buttons to push to make her angry, hurt, and confused? Kat flipped her book open and said sardonically, "That's like the pot calling the kettle black. Don't trip over that big ol' ego of yours in the dark."

"Sleep well, Kat Woman," he said as he walked away. "And don't shoot any more stars out."

Kat loved the dawn, with its magical light, its stillness, its slow slide into sunshine. She'd always had to keep night owl hours because of the circus routines—most days started with an afternoon show and ended after midnight—and wrestling schedules were just as bad.

But after she moved here for good she was never going to miss another dawn. When she settled down. *Some day.* The story of her life. *Some day.*

But today she was going to take another shot at enjoying the stream. Kat trudged along wearing a Wild Women of Wrestling T-shirt over a black swimsuit. Across her shoulder she carried a cloth tote filled with a towel, soap, and shampoo.

She managed without the aid of her crutch, catching low tree branches for support. Finding a spot where the stream bank was flat and sandy, she kicked her Reeboks off and carefully set them in the fork of a tree.

Good running shoes were her one indulgence, and for all she knew, wild critters might like the taste of them.

A deep, musical voice cascaded through the quiet. Kat gasped, looked around, saw nothing, then stood rock-still, listening intently. The voice was Nathan's . . . but he wasn't speaking English.

The words were soft and rolling, the vocal equivalent of water bubbling over rocks in the stream. It was the most ethereal sound she'd ever heard, and it made her shiver with emotion.

Was it some Indian language? And if it was, where had he learned it? And where the heck *was* he?

She edged onto the sandy bank and craned her head around a huge laurel bush which hung over the water. Peeking through the big, oblong leaves, she saw Nathan upstream, his back turned toward her, his hands raised to the sky, his body newborn naked.

If he was some sort of nature worshipper, he certainly had a head start on being natural.

Kat stepped back from the stream, her heart pounding. Whatever he was saying, it appealed to her on a subconscious level that wouldn't let her walk away. Listening to it there in the midst of the land her Cherokee ancestors had loved for centuries, she felt as if she'd slipped through a gateway in time.

A bird sang sweetly nearby. For a second Kat was certain that she had only to look around to find her great-great-grandmother smiling at her.

She trembled and didn't look. Kat shook her head, a little frightened by the intensity of her imagination. Abruptly Nathan stopped talking, and the morning returned to normal.

Kat stood there, wide-eyed, and debated her next move. Oh hell, she might get in trouble, but she couldn't leave without taking another look at him. She inched forward.

He was washing, legs braced apart, arms lifted as he scrubbed each armpit with cheerful vigor. He threw the soap into the air, then whooped as he leapt up and caught it before splashing back down.

Next he bent over and dunked his whole head in the icy stream. Slinging his dark brown hair lustily, he whooped again. Good heavens, he made washing an athletic event.

And she was certainly ready to cheer.

Ordinarily Kat thought naked men looked too vulnerable, like newly hatched chickens who'd been happier before they left their shells. Growing up, she'd glimpse a few bare male essentials, but they belonged to circus performers who were hurrying from one costume into another without caring who watched.

Naked men with names like Blinko the Clown had not exactly been heart-stopping.

Of course, she'd seen her husband naked, but he'd never seemed comfortable either. Without clothes he always seemed to be tiptoeing, even when he wasn't moving. He didn't feel important without his designer underwear and custom-made suits, she'd decided.

But Nathan Chatham looked not only important, he looked positively thrilled to be stark naked in the middle of a stream. Speaking of which—what was that on his right cheek? Some sort of tattoo? Yes!

Kat leaned forward, peering intently. She couldn't make it out, but it was at least three inches long. Wasn't putting a decoration on that fantastic male fanny a lot like gilding a lily?

She'd give anything to know what the tattoo said. Then he turned around and she made a soft squeaking sound of admiration.

All men were not created equal, and the tattoo probably said, "Satisfaction guaranteed."

He was now lathering his hair forcefully, with great white suds falling on his chest and slithering downward, until all Kat could think of was a tree in the middle of a snowbank. A giant sequoia.

She pressed her hands to her mouth to keep from grinning ridiculously. It was only fair that she enjoy this show, after the show he'd had yesterday. Oh, she'd pay for this later in unfulfilled fantasies, but at least her fantasies would be a heck of a lot more exciting than usual.

Nathan bent forward, doused his head so long that she was afraid he might drown, splashed water all over himself, then stood up and looked straight at her laurel bush.

"Good morrrning, Kiiitty Kat," he called in a quaint voice.

She almost lost her balance and fell into the laurel. There was no point in pretending that she wasn't there, so she confronted this humiliation head-on, the way she handled most problems.

"Hi." She stepped into the stream and waved. "Turn on the hot water, would you?"

He put his hands on his hips and confirmed her impression that he was totally comfortable being naked. In fact, he was a lot more comfortable naked than she was in her T-shirt and swimsuit, at the moment.

And he'd accused *her* of being an exhibitionist!

"It's not nice to spy on Mother Nature," he called sternly. "Next time either walk away or join me."

Kat wished she knew some obscene Indian sign language. "This is my stream and my woods and if you want to act like a waterbug, I guess I can stand anywhere I want to and watch you."

"Peeking through leaves is not the most mature thing to do."

"Any man with a lick of sense wouldn't expose himself like some sort of pervert when he *knows* a stranger might be watching."

The dark brows shot up. "Pervert?" he echoed grimly. "You put on a leather bikini and wrestle women in front of an audience and then call *me* a pervert?"

He waded to the bank, snatched a big white towel off a tree branch, slung it around his waist, and started downstream with long, purposeful strides. "If you really think I'm a pervert, then *run*."

Kat stared at him in horror. Old memories stirred an irrational amount of fear inside her suddenly.

What did she know about this man? Practically nothing.

He was at least a head taller than she, and that body had much more than an average share of muscle, stamina, and quickness. Plus, she could barely walk, much less run to save herself. If he weren't trustworthy, if he took her banter as an invitation . . .

She dived for the sandy bank with a force that sent tremors of agony through her ankle. Kat scrambled upright and pushed into the undergrowth blindly, overcome by a panic that numbed her senses.

She didn't know where Nathan Chatham was; she hardly knew where she was, and she didn't care what she might be doing to her fractured ankle. She grabbed a spindly tree for support and went down in a heap when the sapling snapped.

A hand latched onto her shirt. She screamed, twisted onto her back, and looked up into Nathan's severe frown. He held the towel around his waist with one hand; the other let go of her T-shirt and grasped her wrist firmly.

She realized that she was holding both hands up in a desperate and pathetic attempt to ward him off. Stars burst in front of her eyes because she was hyperventilating badly. "Don't," she gasped out. "Please, don't."

He got down on his knees, still holding her wrist, still frowning. She scrambled backward, digging her heels and elbows into prickly vines that a small part of her mind recognized as briars. He wouldn't let go of her wrist.

"Don't, okay? Please?" Kat begged, and burst into tears. That release of energy cleared her head a little, and she finally realized that he was talking to her.

"Dear God. It's all right, Kat, it's all right," he was crooning. "I'm not going to do anything to you. Sssh. I'm not going to attack you. I swear."

She was breathing so raggedly that air barely seemed to be getting past her throat. "Really?"

"Really," he said in a gruff voice. "I never thought you'd suspect me of—Katie, relax. Relax, gal, it's me. You know I wouldn't hurt you."

Katie. What was so calming about that nickname? And about the way he said *It's me,* as if she'd known all along but simply forgotten?

Kat cried harder. What was happening to her? Was she so stressed out from the odd turn her life had taken lately that she was imagining things?

"Kat, calm down," he murmured. He let go of her wrist and held his hand up in a soothing gesture. "Breathe. Breeeathe. Slowly. Slooowly. There. Breathe."

He coached her for at least a minute, his hand poised over her as if he were pressing air into her lungs with gentle insistence. The world came back to life. She stopped crying and her chest no longer felt like a bellows being pumped by a maniac.

Her ankle was a ball of throbbing pain, and the rest of her felt like a pin cushion from her mad dash into a patch of briars. "J—jeez," she managed shakily. "You m-must think I'm a n-nut."

But he was looking at her only with sympathy. He cleared his throat and said hoarsely, "No, I think something pretty awful happened to you once and you thought it was about to happen again."

Oh Lord, he was too perceptive. She nodded weakly, and embarrassment made her skin burn.

"Kat, I'm so sorry for scaring you," he said raspily. "I just wanted to see you squirm."

"Squirm." She managed a small smile. "And I *scrammed.*"

He sat back on his heels and she finally noticed that beneath the towel his legs were covered in bloody scratches. The man had run not only bare-legged but barefoot into a patch of briars to stop her self-destructive stampede.

"Damn, Nathan, I'm sorry. This is awful."

But his attention was focused on her badly swollen ankle. "You really were hurt the other night. Why didn't you say so?"

"Pride," she murmured, and sat up. Briars clung to her. "You made fun of me."

He looked at her from under his brows, conveying so much anguish and regret in his gray eyes that she reached out and patted his jaw. He had a long briar scratch on it.

"You got hurt because you defended me," he noted.

"Uhmmm, we're not supposed to let the audience get beaten up."

He pointed to her ankle. "Did you lose your job because of this?"

"Nah. I can go back when it heals. It's just a fracture. It doesn't even need a cast."

He knelt there looking more and more upset. Kat shifted awkwardly and began pulling briars out of her hair.

"Easy. Be still." He knotted the towel tighter around his waist and went to work on the briars, gently freeing her. "I'm not going to hurt you."

He said it several more times, until finally she assured him softly, "I know that now, Nathan. I just freaked out for a minute. I'm okay. I'm not afraid of you anymore."

"When did someone attack you?" he asked grimly, tugging a briar away from her arm.

"A long time ago. I was twenty. It was somebody I knew, somebody my parents knew. I'd grown up with him. He worked for the circus."

"Circus?"

"I thought you had a line on everything about me and my cousins."

He shook his head. "Only your recent history."

"I was born and raised with the Sheffield Brothers Circus."

"This guy . . ."

"He liked to brag that he turned girls into women. Only I wasn't ready to turn, at least not with him."

"Did you report him to the police?"

She shook her head. "Local cops don't care what

happens among circus people. They wouldn't have believed I was raped. I couldn't tell my family, either. They'd have killed the guy."

Nathan sighed heavily, dropped his hands against his thighs, and looked at her with distress in his sweet, lazy eyes. "It must have been worse than you're making it sound if it still affects you like this."

"It doesn't haunt me anymore. No, I just—" She really didn't want to hurt Nathan's feelings, so she searched for the right words. "I've never been in a situation like this one before. Alone with somebody sort of unpredictable . . . like you."

"Great," he said in weary self-rebuke. "I love knowing that I'm the only man who's terrorized you into hysteria."

His reaction made her catch her breath for new reasons. This man might be dangerous in some ways, but he was a gentleman in the best sense of the word. Kat punched his shoulder playfully. "I'm okay. And, hey, now I'm not afraid of you at all. I trust you. You could run naked around my tent and I wouldn't worry."

He raised a finger and wagged it in mock reproach. "You know, I'm not sure I like this other extreme, either."

As he continued to pull briars away, Kat moved her injured leg tentatively. She was vaguely aware of Nathan Chatham's eyes catching her attempts not to wince with pain. "I'll pay for freaking out," she muttered. "I bet I added about a week to my recuperation."

"Katie, you're a hell of a gal." He stroked his fingertips over the swollen ankle, and she tensed up, expecting the touch to aggravate her pain. Instead the throbbing eased a little.

Katie. Gal. She liked his touch and she liked the way he talked. Again she got the odd notion that she'd always liked these things. Kat gazed at him in awe. "A minute ago why did you say, 'It's me. You know I wouldn't hurt you.' I mean, we're strangers."

He stopped, frowned thoughtfully, and shook his head. "Hmmm. I don't know why I put it that way. I guess I don't think of you as a stranger."

They shared a puzzled look. Kat exhaled slowly and glanced around at huge, gnarled oaks and early morning shadows. "This is a weird place. Good weird. It makes weird things happen."

"How weird," he said drolly.

She cut her eyes at him. "I've got a better vocabulary inside my head. I just don't always use it."

Nathan smiled and carefully picked the last briar from her legs. "Let's see if we can get you out of here." He helped her up, then lifted her into his arms.

Kat's heart rate accelerated with a pleasant kind of excitement when she found herself nestled against his hard, sweaty chest. She latched her hands behind his neck and tried to look everywhere but into his eyes.

He stepped out of the briar patch and started in the opposite direction from her camp. "I live that way," she said, pointing over his shoulder.

Nathan halted and gazed at her worriedly. "I have some ice left in a cooler. I'm going to put it on your ankle and make you some breakfast."

"Ah." She felt guilty. He looked as if she'd accused him of evil designs again. Kat smiled at him. "Okay."

After he started forward she searched for neutral conversation. "That stuff you were saying before you took your bath. Was that some kind of Indian language?"

"Yep." He hesitated a moment. "Cherokee."

"It was?" Kat forgot any awkwardness and studied him curiously. "Are you part Cherokee?"

"Nope. But I grew up in Arkansas, right next door to the reservation in Oklahoma. I was like a grandson to an old medicine man. He adopted me."

"Is that why Tri-State sent you down here? 'Cause you're interested in Cherokee stuff?"

He didn't answer for a minute. "I know a lot about the Oklahoma Gallatins, yeah."

Kat squirmed with excitement and craned her head so that she could gaze directly into his eyes. "You do? See, my cousins and I only know that our great-great-grandma lived here in Georgia. Granny was an Indian named Katlanicha Blue Song and Grandpa was a white guy named Justis Gallatin."

She gripped Nathan's shoulders. "You mean they ended up in Oklahoma? Like they went on the Trail of Tears or something? Have you ever heard of Holt Gallatin? He was their son and my great-grandfather. I think he was a bandit. That's all anybody ever told me."

Overwhelmed by her torrent of words, Nathan stopped. His silver gaze held hers without flinching. Finally he sighed as if resigned and said, "I know about him. He killed two of my relatives."

Three

He walked on calmly, as if he hadn't just announced that her great-grandfather was a killer.

"He did *what*?" Kat asked, stunned.

"Holt Gallatin ambushed my great-great-grandfather outside a saloon and shot him in the back. Gallatin went into hiding and never came back. It was decades before my great-grandfather caught up with him, and then they killed each other in a gunfight."

Kat clung to Nathan's neck, feeling dazed. He chuckled grimly. "You're digging your claws into me, Kitty Kat."

"Sorry. I'm just in shock. Are you sure that my great-grandpa went around blasting people?"

Nathan nodded. His arms tightened under her as he hopped gingerly from one foot to the other. "Ouch. Dammit."

Kat realized with a pang of guilt that he hadn't bothered to get his shoes before carrying her through the forest. "Let me down. I can walk."

"Nope."

"I don't think you like me anymore. I don't want to be a lot of trouble."

He rolled his eyes at her accusation and kept going. "You weren't responsible for our families' feud."

"It was a feud? Over what?"

"An old grudge that started during the Civil War. My great-great-grandpa Nathaniel was a Union officer; your great-great-grandpa Justis was Confederate. Mine caught yours, yours escaped, and mine got demoted because of it. He was disgraced. He resigned from a career in the army because of the scandal."

"But that didn't have anything to do with Holt Gallatin. That escape was his father's doing. Besides, why would the Gallatins want revenge on the Chathams if Justis Gallatin *got away*?"

"We never figured that out. Holt was just the type to pick fights without much reason, according to historical accounts."

"You mean somebody wrote this story down?"

He nodded. "One of my great-uncles researched it for a book. It was published about twenty years ago by the University of Oklahoma Press."

"What's it called? Can I get a copy?"

"Sure. The title's *Blue Fox, Cherokee Renegade*."

Kat drew back and looked at him askance. "That doesn't sound very fair-minded, especially if a Chatham wrote it. Who's Blue Fox?"

"That was the Indian name Holt Gallatin took during the Civil War. He was just a kid, but he killed a Union soldier so that his father—Justis—could escape from my great-great-grandfather."

"Now wait a minute. There was a war goin' on. Justis was supposed to escape if he got a chance. Holt was only doing what everybody else was doing—protecting his family. You can't blame my relatives for disgracing ol' Nath—you're named after him?"

"Yeah."

"Hmmm. This is a real personal thing with you, then, right?"

"I'm not a fanatic about it. I'm just a history buff."

"Uh-huh," she answered in a dubious tone.

They reached a small clearing about a dozen yards from the stream. Kat gaped at the large majestic structure that sat there. "A tipi!"

"Let me guess. You saw one once on television."

Kat gave him a sour look. "You're turnin' ornery again."

He smiled wickedly. "It comes and goes."

"For somebody who blames an Injun for knocking off his relatives, you sure do like Injun stuff a lot."

"My family never blamed Holt Gallatin because he was an Indian; they blamed him because he was a mean hellion." Nathan nodded toward the tipi. "By the way, that's not what Cherokees used to live in; only the nomadic tribes used tipis. That one was a gift from some Sioux friends of mine."

"Don't lecture me," she said quaintly, raising her chin. "I know that the Cherokees lived in little huts. Later on they learned to build cabins and houses."

"Why, you've been reading up a frenzy. You might even learn something."

She glared mildly at him. Smiling a little, he set her down on a folded blanket beside the circle of rock that held the dead embers from his campfire. Kat was too distracted to pay much attention to anything around her; while he went inside his tipi she stared at the charred wood and mulled over everything he'd told her.

Was she really the great-granddaughter of a murderer? The thought depressed her; she'd been so excited when she finally started studying her Cherokee legacy, and now, to find out that Holt Gallatin had been some awful character who went around calling himself Blue Fox and shooting Chathams, well, it made her remember ugly things her husband had said, things about her being low-class.

"Here. The last of the ice from my cooler."

Nathan had traded the towel for his khaki hiking shorts, Kat noted thankfully. Lean and bronzed and too sexy for her to feel at ease, he sat down by her feet, holding ice wrapped in something white. The gold stud gleamed at the top of his ear. Wait a minute. It was no ordinary stud, it was a tiny rough nugget, sort of a miniature of the nugget he wore on the chain.

He pushed a hand through his dark brown hair to guide the drying strands into a vague imitation of obedience, then gently pressed the ice pack to her ankle. Kat watched his face in profile, studying the handsome, crooked nose, the provocative mouth, the thick mustache.

What in the world was she doing anywhere *near* this man? One second he made her want to hold him like a long-lost lover; the next he told her that her family was no-good from way back. Considering what he thought of her work and her lack of sophistication, he must figure that she was worthless.

"I wish you could meet my cousins," she said coolly. "Tess is a diamond broker. She lives on a sailboat. She graduated from college and she has an English accent. Her mother was an Olympic skier from Sweden."

Nathan looked at her with one brow arched, as if she'd lost a few marbles. "That's nice."

"And my cousin Erica owns her own construction company up in Washington. She was born in *Boston*."

"Uh-huh." He turned his attention back to her ankle, patting the ice bag more firmly into place and then cupping his hands around it.

Kat frowned at his lack of response. "So why'd Tri-State send you here if you don't like us Gallatins?"

"Because I'm their best gunslinger. Who said I don't like Gallatins? I just take a lot of pride in my family and I wanted to meet Holt Gallatin's descendants."

"Now wait a minute. Erica's great-granddaddy was Ross Gallatin; Tess's was Silas Gallatin. Ol' Justis and Katherine had three sons. I'm the only one related directly to Holt."

He sighed dramatically. "You've got my sympathy."

Kat jerked her foot away. The ice pack fell off and unrolled before he could catch it. She gazed at it in consternation. It was made from a pair of white briefs. *His underwear.*

"I don't let many woman wear my underwear on their feet," he quipped. "Don't pass up the thrill of a lifetime."

"Look, sweetcakes, you and me don't do so well together. I'm going back to my own camp."

"Nope. You can't walk." He deftly grabbed her big toe. "Stretch that leg out again."

"Let go of my toe!"

"Did anyone ever tell you that you're moody?"

"I don't know what kind of revenge you want to take on us Gallatins, but you can't bully me."

He looked at her through half-shut, guarded eyes. "Revenge? What makes you think I'm not simply doing my job for Tri-State?"

"Oh, sure, you hate my family, so you just happen to wrangle an assignment to do tests on our land." She shook a finger at him. "You'll go to your boss and tell him that there's no gold here. Well, me and my cousins think there is, okay? Lots of it. We've got medallions that were probably made from gold that came from here. I showed mine to somebody who makes jewelry and he said it was the highest-quality gold he'd ever seen."

Nathan stroked his mustache and smiled at her patiently. "I thought you weren't interested in leasing the land to be mined."

"Well, we probably won't. But don't you lie about what you find!"

His smile hardened. "I wouldn't do that. We already suspect that there's industrial-grade gold here. If there's something better, I'll find it and write an honest report."

"Good!"

This didn't make any sense, which was an indication of how much Nathan Chatham rattled her mind. She didn't want to see this land torn up by a mining company, but she was hotly accusing him of intending to ruin a mining deal.

"Let go of my toe," she ordered.

"Nope." He curved his fingers toward her instep. "Ticklish?"

When he smiled wider, she knew he'd read the answer on her face. "I don't know whether you're a devil or a saint, you pierced-ear white Injun," she said lethally. "But don't you mess with me."

"You sit still, you wild-eyed Kat Woman, and let this ice do some good on your ankle. You may not like my company, but you don't want to risk making your ankle any worse. Right?"

She gritted her teeth. "Right."

"Good. Now I'll make breakfast, and you behave."

Smiling benignly, he released her toe and began stirring the embers of his campfire. Suddenly he reached over and smeared a handful of cold ashes on her scratched shins.

She yelped. "What are you doing?"

"Indian medicine," Nathan said solemnly. He scooped up more ashes and held them out to her. "Want to do your thighs without my help?"

Kat sighed with defeat and put her hands out for the ashes. "My thighs don't need your help."

"Think of me as a doctor."

"A witch doctor."

He poured the ashes into her cupped palms. "We're doing a good job of carrying on the Chatham-Gallatin feud. It ought to make you feel proud."

"You bet." Kat's determination flared, and she suddenly felt protective of her family history, no matter how many lawless Blue Foxes it contained. *No Chatham was going to have the last victory.*

She woke up to the feel of a hand stroking her

hair. It dawned on her slowly that the hand belonged to Nathan, but she didn't open her eyes or rebuke him. Instead she curled cozily on her side and pretended to snooze for another second.

Kat refused to consider that she'd fallen asleep as soon as she lay down on the air mattress he'd put beside his campfire for her, or that she'd smiled groggily when he'd covered her in one of his blankets as protection against the cool morning. She was injured, scratched, and emotionally exhausted; she was also wonderfully stuffed from breakfast. She deserved to be helpless for a little while.

But if this was the way he intended to fight the feud, she'd already lost.

He kept stroking her hair, cupping his hand over the top of her forehead and drawing it slowly downward. Kat felt him lift her hair and knew that he was smoothing it out behind her. Then he returned to caressing it.

She was glad he didn't know that he was petting a woman who relaxed like a boneless chicken whenever anyone fiddled with her hair.

Kat supposed that the weight of it made her scalp more sensitive than most people's, more receptive to touch. At any rate, the few times she'd had her hair done in salons she'd dozed blissfully through the wash, trim, and blow-dry, much to the amusement of the stylists.

"Wake up, Kat Woman," he said softly.

Kat sighed and yawned. "I can't. I was drugged with fried trout and biscuits covered in gravy."

"I think you ought to go put your foot in the stream. Cold running water would do it good."

"I can't think of anything I'd like better than to stick my foot in ice water. Go away."

"Kat, it's for your own good."

Suddenly she had no blanket. Suddenly two brawny hands were under her arms, helping her sit up. Her hair fell across her face and got sucked into her mouth when she inhaled. She sputtered and pawed at it.

Nathan Chatham's low chuckle only added to her problems. If he combined that rumbling sound with a scalp message, she'd probably just dissolve into his arms like melted butter.

"Here. Let me." He pushed her hair aside and cupped her face between his hands.

The feel of his calloused fingers and palms made her eyes open wide, banishing sleep. He gazed down at her with quiet, intense scrutiny. "Where'd you get those green eyes?"

"I guess from great-great-grandpa. He was the only white man in my branch of the family. I've heard that my father had green eyes."

"Didn't you know your father?"

"Nope. He and my mother were killed in a train wreck during a circus tour. I was only four. I was adopted by the Flying Campanellis."

"The what?"

"The Flying Campanellis. Italian trapeze artists."

He groaned. "No wonder you don't know anything about your Cherokee background. You're Italian."

She grinned. "*Si. Capisce?*"

Nathan looked at her sadly. "I apologize for making fun of your cultural ignorance."

"Thank you," she murmured softly.

"*Wado,*" he answered.

"Hmmm? Wad what?"

"It means 'thank you' in Cherokee. Say it."

"*Wado.*"

"Now say this." He reeled off a short, musical sentence.

She echoed it carefully. "What did I say?"

He smiled. "Something on a par with 'You're the best-looking man I've ever seen.' "

Kat's lips parted in a soft sigh, and his gaze dropped to them. She couldn't think straight yet, and he was taking advantage. "I was duped. I meant to say, 'Which way to the stream?' "

He helped her to her feet, then scooped her into his arms again. Kat was very aware of his forearm nestling under her bare thighs. Her T-shirt had ridden up on her stomach to show her pelvis covered in a clingy black swimsuit cut high on the sides.

At the risk of revealing her dismay, she tugged the bottom of her T-shirt down as far as it would go.

He pursed his lips coyly. "An attack of modesty, Princess Talana?"

"You were looking at my thighs like Colonel Sanders eyeing a chicken dinner."

"Make that a Cajun dinner. You're covered in so much soot that you look like a blackened redfish." He paused. "A blackened redskin, I mean."

She chortled and covered her lips, disgusted with his easy control over her humor. "You carry squaw to water," she ordered.

Nathan headed toward the stream a few yards away. "Don't use words like that. 'Squaw' is insulting. Back in the old days Cherokee women were a powerful force in the tribe. They had complete control over the children and the households. They had a say on the councils. A Beloved Woman could free prisoners taken in battle. All she had to do was step forward and touch them with a swan feather."

"What's a Beloved Woman?"

"Someone special, someone the tribe respected. A wise counselor."

"So I shouldn't say 'squaw' anymore, huh?"

"Not if you want to show people that you respect your heritage."

"Okay. No more squaw."

He sat her down on the stream bank so that her feet dangled in the cold, rushing water. Kat shivered. "I feel the fracture healing in self-defense."

"Say this." Nathan smiled ruefully. "We'll use English so you won't suspect me of being bad. 'Listen!' "

"Okay."

"No, say it. 'Listen!' "

"Listen!"

"You have drawn near to hear me, Grandfather Moon."

She repeated the sentence obediently.

"My name is Katlanicha. I am of the blue clan."

"Look, I was named after my great-great-grandmother *Katherine*—"

"Who's the doctor here, you or me? Her Cherokee name was Katlanicha, so *your* name is Katlanicha."

Kat huffed with mock disgust. "My name is Katlanicha. I am of the blue clan."

"You have come to carry my pain away, Grandfather Moon. And now relief is here. Listen!"

She repeated everything he'd told her.

Nathan nodded with approval. "Say that formula each time you soak your foot in the stream."

"Oh, I see. You're just like every other doctor. 'Take two formulas and call me in the morning.' "

Nathan shot her an amused, exasperated look. "Are you going to be difficult to teach?"

"Who said you're teaching me?"

"You want to feel that you belong on this Cherokee land?"

"Yeah." Her teasing attitude faded. "More than anything," she whispered.

He took her hand and kissed it jauntily. "Then hang around with me, Katlanicha Gallatin."

Kat smiled. That was the best invitation she'd ever heard. Shrugging, she said, "Sure. I guess I can put up with a Chatham."

Nathan took a drag on his pipe and squinted through the firelight at her tent, which he'd insisted on moving to his own campsite. It sat about twenty feet from his tipi, on the other side of the fire, as if the fire were a dividing point between two enemy factions.

She stepped out of her tent, looked a little startled

to see him staring straight at her, and smiled crookedly. "You afraid I'll scalp you when you turn your back'?"

"Nah. Music soothes the savage wrestler."

He laid his pipe down on one of the rocks that circled the fire, then picked up a foot-long harmonica. Her green eyes wide with amusement, she limped to the fire and sat down gingerly, then wrapped her hands around one updrawn knee.

"So blow, Chatham."

Nathan pretended to be thinking about his selection as his gaze roamed over her—her beautiful, athletically sculpted legs revealed to the upper thighs by cut-off jeans, her bare feet looking delicate and kissable, her breasts outlined by some sort of sheer bra that didn't hide much under her white T-shirt.

"What kind of music do you like?" he asked, shifting in an effort to ease the very masculine response in his body.

She smiled with a shyness that surprised him. "Opera."

Nathan nearly dropped the harmonica. "Nah."

"Yeah." She nodded fervently. "It's crazy, I know. But Papa Campanelli was really into it, and I learned from him." She lifted her chin. "Ask me anything about Puccini. Go ahead."

"When I think of something, I'll let you know."

"You like opera?"

Nathan laughed softly. "Lady Savage with her pointed bra and cow horns is my idea of opera."

"You've never heard of *La Bohème*?"

"Not unless it hit the Top Forty. I'm a radio man, mostly."

"Oh, you don't know what you're missing." She reached into the air, gesturing vigorously. "The drama, the excitement, the passion!"

"Sounds like a wrestling match. That why you like wrestling so much?"

She cut her eyes at him. "I like to pay my bills."

"So how long are you going to wrestle? Until they call you 'Princess Toothless Talana'?"

She flung a twig at him. "Maybe I'll get to be a star some day, like Hulk Hogan, and make a lot of money."

"If you turn into Hulk Hogan you're gonna have a lot of disappointed men in the audience."

"Huh." She ducked her head, idly fiddled with the elastic bandage on her foot, and said, "You ever been married, harmonica man?"

"Nope. Traveled too much. Spent too much time in places where even kissing a woman was a dangerous thing."

"Why dangerous?"

"Well, depending on which tribe it was, I'd either have to marry her and all her sisters, kill myself, sacrifice a goat to the gods, or donate part of my anatomy to her upset daddy." He arched a brow. "I didn't like the options."

Laughing, she rocked back and forth, the firelight soft and inviting on her. "You must be glad to be home."

"Oh, I don't know. It's not always safe to kiss women here, either."

"What do they do?"

"I don't know. Been so long I've forgotten."

"Oh sure."

"Really." He clasped his chest and tried to look needy. "I could use a refresher course."

She'd been grinning at him. Slowly the grin faded to a polite smile. She looked away and said softly, "Play that harmonica for me."

Nathan winced inwardly. He'd probably scared her so much the other day that she wouldn't forget easily. Every time she thought he was interested, she retreated.

"I don't know any opera," he said. "How about this?"

He put the instrument to his lips and played a soft, sweet blues tune. Nathan focused his gaze on the fire as he played, but he felt her watching him, and that made concentration difficult. When he finished he looked over to find her lips parted seductively, as if she'd been thinking how his mouth would feel on something other than a harmonica.

"Ever tried it?" he asked gruffly. Nathan wiped the mouthpiece and offered the harmonica to her.

She pressed it to her mouth and looked at him expectantly. A rivulet of hot sensation wound through him at the idea of her lips and tongue caressing the same metal.

"Just play with it," he urged. "See what kinds of sounds you can make."

For a minute she toyed with the harmonica, laughing at the squawks and squeaks it produced, smiling when more pleasant notes came out. "Here. I'm impressed," she said finally, handing it back. "You make it look easy."

"It's all in the tongue." He put the harmonica to his lips without wiping it. Her eyes flickered with surprise, and she ran a hand over her hair as if stroking it in reaction to some secret, sensual thought.

He had trouble remembering any other songs as he tasted her on the mouthpiece. Lord, he'd never gotten aroused playing the harmonica before. She leaned forward, waiting, and whether the eagerness in her expression was for music or for him, it had an even more disastrous effect on his concentration.

"I have a whole collection of these," he said, lowering the harmonica and gazing at her while his body tightened with a very primitive desire to taste her mouth without the harmonica for a chaperone. "I have a wooden flute and a guitar, too."

She blinked groggily, sat back, and fanned herself with one hand, looking at the fire as if it were the culprit who'd made her too warm. "I think the guitar would be a real good idea."

"Right. I'll go get it." As he walked to the tipi he thought, *No mouths involved.*

They sat side by side on the stream bank, not talking, but not uncomfortable with the silence. It was an amazing thing, Kat thought, for two people who'd known each other only a few days to be able to do this.

He fished, and she read one of her history books. At least, she tried to read. She kept a large part of her mind tuned to him since he was only a foot away and wearing only his hiking shorts.

"Says here," she murmured softly, "that the Indian Territory was a pretty wild place."

He flicked a hook baited with corn into a new spot and said something in Cherokee. When she looked at him quizzically he winked and explained, "You're supposed to apologize to the fish for trying to catch them. That way they won't get mad and leave."

"I've known men who tried to get dates that way."

"Did they?"

"Nope. I swim pretty fast." She cleared her throat. "About the Indian Territory."

"Yeah, it was rough, especially on the border between the Nation and Arkansas. Lots of bandit gangs, not much law. But then there were real nice places in the Nation, too—big farms, towns, schools."

"The Nation?"

"Sure. You call it Indian Territory, but it was made up of separate nations—Cherokee, Creek, Choctaw, Chickasaw, Seminole. The Cherokees had their own government, their own courts."

"Then my great-grandpa should have been caught and tried by his own people, if he was so bad."

"Well," Nathan said in a skeptical tone, "it wasn't that neat. For one thing, he was a Keetowah, and the Cherokees had a lot of respect for them."

"What's a Keetowah?" she asked, fascinated.

"Traditionalist. Secret society. Cherokees who wanted to keep strictly to the old ways. They refused to speak English or go by English names. They wanted all whites kicked out of the Nation."

"But wouldn't that have made Holt an enemy of his own family, since his father was white?"

"Nope. Not unless his father was against Indian ways. Ol' Justis wasn't like that."

"How do you know?"

"Well, I . . ." he paused, thinking as his skilled hands slowly cranked the fishing reel. "I figure any man who married a Cherokee, raised his children in Cherokee ways, and led Cherokee troops in the war must have been Cherokee at heart."

"You know a lot about him."

"Not really. Only what I read in the book my great-uncle wrote. Justis and Katherine had a big farm before the war. Didn't own slaves though, and most of the biggest Cherokee farmers did."

"But Justis was a Confederate officer during the war?"

"Hmmm. A major. Got wounded in the arm when my great-great-grandpa caught him. He got away, but I'd bet gold that he was permanently crippled in that arm. The ammo they used in those days did a nasty job."

Kat slammed her book shut. "Well, no wonder Holt had something against your family!"

"Now look, Kat Woman, my great-great-granddaddy lost two sons who fought for the Union—killed by Confederate troops made up of Cherokees. My relatives got *scalped*, so don't turn self-righteous on me, okay?"

"You hate my family and I'm trying to defend them."

He shook his head, the chocolate-brown hair shagging forward over his forehead. "I don't hate people I never knew."

"You know me!"

"Well, I sure don't hate you."

The fervent way he said that, as if hate weren't even in his vocabulary where she was concerned, made Kat stare at him wistfully. "I don't hate you, either."

An electric silence settled between them as he met her gaze and held it. "Katie," he said in a soft, gruff tone. "I don't think we could ever hate each other."

In her rational mind Kat knew that two people who'd met less than a week ago shouldn't use such certain words, but with his somber gray eyes pouring affection into her all she could think was, *He's right.*

"Would you—" she began.

His fishing rod jerked wildly and he faced forward, struggling with it.

Kiss me, she added silently.

"Got a big one, Kat Woman," he shouted. "Sharpen your claws!"

Sighing, Kat reached for the net behind her. She made a great pal for Nathan, but not much of anything else.

She peered out of her tent the next morning to find the fire burning and a covered pot sitting in the center of it. Sniffing at an unidentifiable but delicious smell, Kat peered around but saw no sign of Nathan. She gazed at his tipi, trying to see inside the dark triangle where the flap was pulled back, and concluded that he wasn't there, either.

Quickly she tugged her sleeping bag outside and sat down on it to do some stretching exercises. Her discipline, developed during years of work with the trapeze performers, had now become a form of meditation. It was difficult to meditate when Nathan was around.

She felt decently covered in a long, loose T-shirt and panties. If Nathan came back from wherever he was, he wouldn't see anything compared to what her

Princess Talana getup had revealed. She wasn't certain what he thought of her, but she didn't want to look like a tease, especially when the teasing didn't seem to do any good.

With a low sigh of delight, Kat spread her legs in a wide split and leaned forward from the waist, feeling well-trained muscles loosen and slide as she flattened herself to the ground. She rested the side of her face on the edge of the sleeping bag and extended both arms in front of her.

She was still in that position several minutes later when she heard the rustling sound of footsteps. Kat propped her chin on one hand and watched as Nathan strode into the clearing, water dripping from his body, his dark hair slicked back, a towel wrapped low around his waist.

All her muscles went on alert. He really knew how to ruin a good meditation.

He halted the second he saw her in her strange contortion on the sleeping bag, and one end of his mustache lifted under a lopsided, devilish smile. She had the notion that he might growl lecherously and head straight for her. The man was full of mischief.

"I have to stretch," she explained firmly. "Or I get cricks."

"Let me see what I can do to help."

Before she could protest he was beside her, kneeling on the sleeping bag, his hands pushing her hair off her back so that he could massage her shoulders. Kat was very aware of how she must look from his angle—her legs spread almost straight out from her body, her rump sticking up a little, covered only by panties and the tail of her T-shirt.

"I didn't figure on this," she muttered.

"Relax, I'm not gawking," he said cheerfully. "I saw more when Lady Savage was holding you over her head."

"Gee, thanks. Hope you got your money's worth."

He patted her shoulder. "You don't have to worry about me, kid. I'm not gonna scare you again."

"Thanks," Kat said grimly. What he really meant was, he wasn't interested in tangling with her.

He molded his hands to her back and stroked them down both sides, kneading her with the tips of his fingers, rubbing small circles on her spine with his thumbs. "You know," he said calmly, "a lot of times our society calls other people primitive because they run around without any clothes. But it seems a hell of a lot more primitive to go around covered up on a pretty summer day like this."

"What did Cherokees wear, before they turned white?"

He chuckled, his fingers still working their magic through the cotton of her T-shirt. "They never turned white. They took up a lot of white ways, but underneath it they were always different."

"Which way?"

"Well, like your great-grandfather. If his own people had arrested him, they wouldn't have put him in jail to wait for trial. He'd just go on about his business and come into court the day he was due. The old ways were based on personal honor."

He rubbed her lower back, pushing down with the palms of his hands, brushing the curve of her hips with his fingertips before he retreated up her spine again. Kat quivered as her body loosened in a way that wanted to welcome him inside.

"You okay?" he asked.

"Hmmm. Yeah, No problem. The, uhmm, the personal honor. More."

Oh, yes. More, Nathan, more.

"Cherokees didn't like to order other people around. Everybody was supposed to know the basic rules of the tribe, but then do their own thing. Not a bad way to live—share what you have, do what you want as long as you don't break the important taboos, respect your elders, be polite to your family."

"What taboos?" Kat asked languidly. She was liquid with heat inside and so mesmerized by his voice and hands that she could barely think.

"Marrying into your own clan, murder, ignoring the mourning rituals after a relative died. And a man, for instance, could get into deep trouble if he abused a woman or child."

"What happened to him?"

"Women from the victim's clan would beat him up."

Kat laughed softly. Oh Lord, Nathan was rubbing the back of her head now. "Cherokee women must have had a lot of power."

"Sure did. They weren't second-class citizens." His voice dropped to a teasing rumble. "But then, women who run around half-dressed can get just about anything they ask for."

This was her chance. Kat raised her head. "Then I'd like—"

"Dammit, my frogs are boiling over!"

He leapt up and ran to the fire. Dazed, Kat pushed herself into a sitting position and stared as he plucked the lid off the pot and stirred the contents with his bowie knife.

"Frogs?"

"Yeah. Bullfrogs. I caught 'em this morning. See, you parboil 'em, then roast 'em. Best frog legs you've ever tasted."

Kat groaned softly and went back in her tent. Between frogs and fish, she'd never get anywhere with Nathan.

They'd been alone together, not having seen another human soul for over a week now. They'd watched hawks, deer, possums, racoons, rabbits, squirrels, and owls, and they'd discussed most of them in detail as to Cherokee name and legends. They were happy without other company.

At least she was happy, Kat corrected herself. And she guessed Nathan was—he never got very far away from her, and he was always concerned about her ankle, and he asked lots of polite questions about her hobbies and ideas. But he didn't flirt very much, and that was making her more miserable with each passing day.

Did she want to get herself in deep water with this man? Yes, deep water in the stream, *nekkid*, and she wanted him to run his hands through her hair and later on show her exactly what was tattooed on his rump.

She sat one afternoon and watched him draw the Cherokee alphabet in the sand for her, with the sunlight glinting on his hair, his body clothed only in those damned sexy buckskin breeches, his muscles flexing under the freckled, richly tanned skin of his back.

His voice was smooth as warm liniment. He was kind and patient, the best teacher in the world. When she asked questions or offered some comment he sat very still and listened, really listened, without making fun of her for being uneducated.

Oh Lord. This was terrible. She was falling in love with him.

Four

He had himself a neighbor, a student, a patient, and a very big problem since he didn't think of Kat as the enemy anymore. In fact, after knowing her for only a week, he wanted to run up the white flag, sign a peace treaty, and give her any territorial right her sweet little heart wanted.

She might talk like a wisecracking truckstop waitress and act as if she didn't care to be sophisticated, but there was a sharp lady under all that fast talk. Her grasp of national and world events would put most people to shame, even though she swore that she got all her information from Oprah and Phil and Geraldo.

Her mind was very quick and as inquisitive as a child's, as a result, he believed, of growing up in the circus. She always had been traveling, always meeting new people and living in new places. Unlike most adults, she'd never fully lost a child's fascination with the world.

She was sincere about learning Cherokee lore, and they spent a lot of their time sitting at the campfire while he talked and she listened, her head tilted to one side, her chin propped on one hand.

She listened the same way whenever he played one of his six harmonicas or his flute or the small guitarlike instrument he'd gotten in South America. They traded stories about his travels as a geologist and her circus experiences and the wrestling tour.

On the other hand, they spent many silent hours together, usually by the stream.

He fished and she read her history books. Periodically she stuck her injured foot in the water and solemnly repeated the formula he'd given her. Now she knew how to say it in Cherokee.

After he'd had time to think about the upsetting scene in the briar patch, he'd continued to keep his flirting lighthearted. Despite her nonchalant assurances that she wasn't afraid of him, she seemed to feel uncomfortable every time he got close.

Lord, he couldn't blame her. The little doll had been through hell—raped at twenty, too scared to fool with men for years after that, then so lonely that she married the first man who made her feel loved and safe.

Nathan had learned enough to know that she'd been married for three years to an ambitious car salesman in Miami. How had she described him? *He just wanted to marry a housekeeper until he could afford to hire one.*

During her marriage the Flying Campanellis had flown back to Italy and joined a circus there, so her divorce two years ago had left her jobless. With no skills outside the circus, she'd decided that professional wrestling was her best opportunity to make a living.

Nathan emptied his pipe into the fire and got up wearily. It wasn't wise for him to get to know Kat so well. He'd been happier thinking of her as a sexy clown with bad taste and no brains. Now he was in a dilemma about the Gallatin land, a dilemma built on promises he'd made to his grandfather. Nothing was ever to happen to the land as long as Dove Gallatin was alive, Grandpa Micah had told him, but after she passed on, the family debt needed to be paid. Grandpa had been an old bastard in some ways—part of the feud was his fault—but in this case he had had a point.

Nathan picked up a bucket and doused the campfire. He stood in darkness lit only by a new moon, gazing at Kat's tent. That activity seemed to be his only hobby these nights. He'd insisted that she keep his air mattress. Injured foot and all that.

Hell, he really just wanted to know that she was lying where he'd lain. Did she sleep naked? He had a disturbing vision of himself affectionately nuzzling his air mattress after she gave it back.

This kind of nonsense had to stop.

He should be discouraging her interest in her Cherokee past and this land. He ought to tell her the ugly details not only about Holt Gallatin but also about Holt's daughter, Dove. Kat's grandfather Joshua had been Dove's brother, so what did that make Dove? Kat's great-aunt?

But Joshua Gallatin had had nothing to do with the Chatham-Gallatin feud. He'd joined the Sheffield Brothers Circus as a kid and left home for good. He'd raised Kat's father in the business, and after her father married a full-blooded Cherokee woman from the reservation up in North Carolina, he'd taken her back to the circus with him.

Kat was born in a circus dressing room, a Cherokee in name only, a damned Gallatin in name only. Kat was innocent. Kat ought not to suffer because of old feuds and old promises.

Nathan rammed his hands through his hair. All right, he had ways to make it up to her—lots of money, more money than she'd ever dreamed possible, and luxuries she couldn't imagine.

After she learned the truth about him and what he intended, he'd show her how generously he could apologize and how effectively he could change her track record with men.

She couldn't go on this way, and yet she never wanted to leave. Kat peeked out of her tent, watching Nathan heat a pot of coffee over the fire. He wore his fringed buckskin breeches, leather hiking boots, and a T-shirt he'd gotten at the Olympics in Korea.

Before going to work for Tri-State the man had hunted for gold all over the world. Now that she knew where and why he'd acquired the tattoo and the pierced ear, she was more fascinated than ever. Kat felt a familiar ache of sadness.

He was friendly, helpful, and very, very kind. He really put her at ease. But then, so did a Boy Scout.

Kat sighed. She didn't want a Boy Scout, she wanted the wicked man from their first encounters. She wanted him to make her forget good sense and indulge the reckless sensations that seethed inside her so much of the time.

She plopped down and slipped her feet into her pink Reeboks, leaving the laces on the one on the bad foot untied. She could walk pretty well now, dammit. There were no excuses for him to carry her anymore.

Leaving her tent, she put on a bright smile. "Morning, harmonica man."

He was already watching her intently from his seat by the fire. Kat shivered inside. If he wasn't interested, why did he study her like some new kind of native each morning when she came out?

"Sleep good, Kitty Kat?"

She smiled at the teasing nickname. It had grown so familiar that she cherished it. "Yeah. But I got a crick in my neck." She rotated her head, making sure her hair slipped forward like a silky black wave. "Would you mind braiding my hair for me? Until my neck loosens up, it would really hurt for me to do it myself."

He hesitated, and Kat's hopes fell. But he cleared his throat, fiddled with the blackened coffeepot, and said lightly, "No problem. Have a cup of tar."

Using a towel, he lifted the steaming metal pot and poured thick black coffee into a metal cup that, thank goodness, had an insulated handle. Kat sat down beside him, put an elastic hair band and brush on the ground, and took the cup carefully.

"Ya know, Nathan, this stuff would make great paint remover."

"It's good for cleaning carburetors, too." He took a swallow from his own cup and made a deep, half-growling sound of satisfaction. "Puts hair on my hair."

"Hair." She smiled sweetly, turned her back to him, and waited.

After a moment his hands slipped over her shoulders and pulled the thick mane back. Kat's eyelids became heavy with a languor that had nothing to do with sleep. Good grief, he'd barely touched her and already a warm, tickling wave of pleasure had begun in her belly.

"Don't ever get this cut," he said gruffly.

"I haven't had it more than trimmed since I was ten years old. It looked real dramatic in the circus act—this little bitty girl with hair longer than she was. So Mama Campanelli said to let it stay that way. 'Course, it really gets attention when I wrestle. Everybody loves it."

"The men in the audience, huh?"

"Well, yeah. It's pretty sexy-looking. I wouldn't be honest if I said I didn't know that."

"How do you feel about the things they yell?"

"I don't much hear 'em." She hesitated for a second. "I guess there are a lot of ugly things I don't want to hear."

He slid his hands down her hair, parting it, lifting

it, winding his fingers through it, and then letting go. Nathan's technique told her a lot about his nature—this was a man who loved to touch. He worshipped her hair, and she suspected that he'd treat the rest of her with the same slow attention.

Kat sighed with pleasure. Asking him to braid her hair was one of the best decisions of her life.

"You don't deserve to have men treat you like a piece of meat," he said grimly.

"Well, long as they're in the audience and I'm in the ring, I just look at it as harmless show biz. They're not drooling at me, they're drooling at Princess Talana."

"You can really separate yourself from it that way?"

"Most of the time," she said softly. "But some nights I feel embarrassed."

"What would you do if you could do anything in the world besides wrestle for a living?"

"I'd teach school," she said immediately. "To me that's the best of both worlds. It's show biz, sort of like wrestling, but it's respectable. And you have to go to college to do it."

When he finished laughing he said, "Kat, I want to be in your class some day."

She grinned. "Teacher's pet."

He ran his fingers through her hair from the crown of her head to the curve of her back, skimming her spine with his fingertips as he did. Kat fought a desire to earn her name by purring.

"You'd make a great hairdresser," she said. "You're awful familiar with the client, though."

His hands halted. "Want me to stop?"

"Not on your life."

"You're one honest woman," he murmured. "I like that."

Kat pursed her lips ruefully. She hadn't been honest about the crick in her neck. With his fingers woven into her hair, she couldn't feel much remorse. "Yeah, I try to tell it like it is."

"So what do you do when people aren't honest back?"

"I drop 'em like hot rocks."

"Hmmm." He kept running his fingers down her hair, slowly, tugging just a little, touching her back just a little, delighting her in ways he probably never suspected. "You don't give people the benefit of the doubt?" he asked softly, stroking the back of her head. "A second chance? Even if they apologize?"

Kat had her eyes shut. Her body hummed with the kind of delicious alertness that made it feel too heavy to move. She had to think hard to get her mouth in gear. "Well, okay, I'm not hard-nosed if somebody really apologizes. Hmmm."

"Nothing hard about you," he agreed. His fingers pressed into her shoulders, massaging. "Where's the crick?"

"Hmmm. That feels good."

Any second now she'd curl around his legs with her back arched.

He picked up the brush and put it at the top of her forehead. Slowly he pulled it back, letting each bristle caress her scalp. Kat's head tilted back loosely.

"What's that?" he asked. "Did I hurt you? You made a noise."

She forced her head forward and tried to control herself. "Nah."

He divided her hair and began to braid it down the center of her back, his fingers skillful and unhurried. Obviously concerned about doing a good job, he stopped frequently to smooth his hand over her head, tickling her earlobes, brushing the edges of her face.

Kat pressed her palms together and found them hot. She had to transfer this heat to Nathan, had to tell him that she adored him and would love to show how much. Surely he found her desirable; he had seemed to at first, before she'd frightened him with the briar incident.

She began to turn her head. "Nath—"

"All done," he said abruptly. With a quick pat on her shoulder, he got up and walked toward the food supplies hanging in a nearby tree. "Let's eat something simple for breakfast. Now that your ankle's better, we ought to start exploring the land."

Kat sagged like a rag doll and braced both hands on the ground beside her. She watched him blankly, a groan of dismay trapped in her throat.

He had to have felt her quivering; he had to have known that she was helplessly desperate for his touch. He was either biding his time to make her crazy, or he was politely ignoring her interest.

Lord, she hoped it was the first one. Kat drank her coffee in several huge gulps. Jolt. Caffeine. Reality. She tried to connect her muscles to her bones again.

Hunched over the net full of supplies, his back to her, Nathan fumbled with various items, his hands trembling. In about five minutes he might be able to walk back to the campfire without revealing how he'd made a new sort of camping tent in the front of his buckskins.

Her hair, that was the key. When she was ready to be seduced, he'd start with her hair.

He frowned at her dedicated attempt at walking, dropped his canvas knapsack, backed up to her, and pointed over his shoulder. "Climb aboard."

"The top of the ridge is just up there."

"Never turn down a free pony ride. Come on."

Kat grinned. What was she, an idiot? "Never." She grasped his shoulders as he reached behind him and scooped his hands around her thighs. Oh yes, she thought, this pony ride was a wonderful idea.

She straddled his lower back, clamped her arms around his neck, and leaned forward just enough to let her breasts brush his shoulders. He groaned loudly as he bent over to pick up the knapsack.

Good. He'd noticed that she had a bosom.

"You're getting heavier," he said in a strained voice. "Here. Take the knapsack."

Kat thought about biting his ear, but decided against it. She had no place to put the knapsack except in front of her chest. She sighed with resignation and wedged it there. "Hike on, mule."

Despite his jovial complaints he easily carried her up the last part of the steep hillside. When they reached the top, sheltered by huge oaks and maples, he turned around. Kat peered over his shoulder at the magnificent valley. She could just make out the stream winding across the far side.

"It's so beautiful it makes me kind of hurt inside," she whispered. "I want to hug it."

"Your great-great-grandmother and her family must have hated to leave here."

"When was it that all the Cherokees got kicked out? I forgot."

"Eighteen thirty-eight. Soldiers and state militia rounded 'em up like animals, and mobs of settlers came along behind taking over the farms and stealing everything that wasn't nailed down."

"Katherine, I mean Katlanicha, met Justis and married him, so we know she survived the Trail of Tears," Kat said softly. "But we figure her family didn't. We don't know anything about them."

Nathan turned around, gazing at the forest. "This timber probably hasn't been touched since the family left. Some of these trees have got to be nearly two hundred years old."

"Dove's will didn't say anything about any of the Gallatins coming back here to live—not in four generations."

"Well, for a long time they wouldn't have been welcome. You know, the only thing that saved this land from being claimed by a white settler was the fact that it was in Justis Gallatin's name. The law said Cherokees couldn't own property in the state of Georgia."

She exhaled heavily. "The world's a crazy place, Nathan."

"Better than it used to be, in some ways." He bounced her a little. "Hang on. I'm going to my truck."

"I still haven't figured how I missed it when I drove in."

"You'll see."

He piggybacked her to the end of a narrow trail just wide enough to drive a car along. He walked past her Mustang and down into a deep hollow on the other side of the trail. There sat a shiny black 4X4 with massive wheels and a black camper hood over the bed.

"Oooh. Lots of chrome. And a gun rack!" Kat noted coyly. "Why, men who drive these kinds of fancy toys are the type who *love* wrestling."

"Hey, only party girls drive Mustangs with bad paint jobs and rusty mag wheels. Party girls with names like 'Beulah Ann' or 'Fanny Mae.' They cruise into town with their beehive hairdos sprayed stiff and they—*yow*. Get your teeth off my ear!"

She eased her teeth from the gold nugget and chuckled victoriously.

Nathan set her down by the truck and glared at her, though his mouth quirked under the mustache. "Hellion."

"Thank you." She blew him a kiss.

The truck had a plush red interior and more gadgets than a gourmet kitchen. He lifted her into the driver's seat so that she could study the cellular phone, state-of-the-art stereo system, and CB radio.

"Where are the flight controls?"

"I love my truck," he said solemnly, and went around back to retrieve something from the camper.

When he returned he held a small shovel and a

long contraption that looked like a Geiger counter on a microphone stand with a dinner plate at the other end. "Metal detector," he told her.

"You use that to find gold? I thought those things found metal only near the top of the ground."

"That's right." He clicked a switch and pointed the plate end toward his truck. Inside a panel on the control box a needle bounced crazily.

"You found it, Nathan. It's a truck all right."

He eyed her with amusement. "I'm not looking for gold with this, I'm looking for evidence of people. Find where the people were and maybe you'll find the sites of old mines. Get it, Kitty Kat?"

"Got it."

"Besides, it's fun to hunt for things in the dirt."

She nodded. "I lost a baby tooth once. I went through a pile of dried elephant manure to get it back. It was worth a quarter from the tooth fairy."

He slid one arm around her waist and pulled her out of the truck, then held her against him and growled with mock lechery, "I could really go for a woman who plays in pachyderm poop."

Kat laughed so hard that she didn't get a chance to protest when he stepped away sooner than she liked. Smiling weakly, she took the shovel and followed him out of the hollow.

Back on top of the ridge he stopped and looked around, squinting his eyes as he thought. "The trees," he said in a soft, fascinated tone. "Hmmm."

Kat gazed at the huge hardwoods with a feeling of awe. "This would be a great place to build a house. With the valley in front and a big, flat ridge in back. There's room for barns and stuff up here, too."

"Exactly." Nathan pointed toward the valley. "The trees down there are younger than these. I bet that whole valley used to be farmland. And up here—" He looked around, his gray gaze searching, excited.

"Turn on the metal detector," Kat urged.

"Easy, gal. There are dozens of places on this land

where the Blue Song family might have built. And they most likely didn't have anything fancy."

"But this is where the trail comes in from the road," she pointed out. *Gal.* It was a good sign when he said *gal.* "Let's look around."

He switched the metal detector on and they started across the ridge. Nathan swung the detector in a slow arc as they walked, while Kat hobbled along with the shovel poised for digging.

"How's your ankle?" he murmured, his eyes on the ground.

"Fine. Everything's nice and flat up here."

"Put your shovel at ease, soldier. Save your energy."

"I *know* we're going to find something."

But an hour later they were still crisscrossing the ridge without success. The plan didn't seem nearly so easy to Kat now. Her ankle had started to throb.

"Want to call it a day?" Nathan asked.

"Just a few minutes more. Let's go back toward the front."

They ambled along. She began using the shovel like a cane. Nathan stopped, frowning. "Time to quit. You need to go soak that foot."

"Relax, Mommy, I'm fine." She pointed the shovel toward a little clearing a few yards away. "Let's go over there."

"Nope. This is like eating popcorn. At some point you just have to say, 'I'm stopping for now' and then—Kat, come on back. Kat, give it up for today."

"Nope." She limped toward the clearing.

"I'm not following."

"Yeah, you are too."

His voice rose. "*Katlanicha.*"

The way he said her full name made an odd feeling wash over her. She kept walking and called, "Sir, you need to indulge me on this."

Sir, you need to indulge me on this?

Where had that come from? She'd never said anything so formal-sounding in her whole life.

Well, it worked, at any rate. She turned around and found Nathan striding toward her, looking very exasperated, the metal detector gripped tightly in one hand. He raised the other hand and shook his finger at her.

"*Katie Blue Song, I've told you before that—*"

He stopped, frowning deeply. They stared at each other. "Told me what?" Kat asked, while the odd feeling grew more potent inside her. "Katie Blue Song?"

Nathan shook his head. "I don't know what I was going to say." He glanced down at the metal detector and his mouth opened in shock.

Kat almost fell down hurrying to cover the yard of leafy ground that separated them. Her heart racing, she looked at the detector's needle.

It was going wild.

Five

Kat jabbed the shovel into the ground, barely missing the toe of his hiking boot. He jumped.

"Take it easy," Nathan urged. "We have a lot of
work to do. Go slow and steady."

"I can't!" She tried to balance on her good foot and
push the shovel with her injured one; the pain was
too great. She levered all her upper-body weight on
the shovel and managed to sink it only a few inches
into the soft humus. "Arrrgh."

Chuckling, Nathan took the shovel away. "You look
like a little brown hen trying to scratch a hole in
concrete. Take the metal detector and let me dig."

She grabbed the detector and circled him, watching the needle. Kat was so excited she wasn't sure
which was shaking harder—she or the indicator.
"There's something. And there. And there. More.
Yes! Oh, Nathan, Yes! More!"

"Yes, more, oh, Nathan, more," he muttered.
"Women are never satisfied." Shaking his head in
mock disgust, he shoveled leaves and dirt aside.

Kat laughed giddily and ranged farther, yipping
each time the needle danced. "What do you think
we've found?"

"Who knows? Keep track of your area. Try to find the perimeter."

Whump. "Ouch! Dammit!"

"What'd you do?"

"Ran into a tree." Smiling sheepishly, she rubbed her forehead and kept walking.

He choked back laughter. "Kitty Kat, look up every once in a while."

Now she hurt at both ends, but she hardly noticed. With adrenaline firing her energy, she swung the metal detector and watched the needle carefully.

Fifteen minutes later she made her way back to Nathan. He'd dug a square hole about five feet wide and a foot deep.

"Why aren't you finding anything?" she asked plaintively.

"Patience, gal, patience."

Gal. Yes, a very good sign. He'd probably find something any minute. Kat pointed at the surrounding woods. "The needle stops moving when I get past that big oak over there, that maple over there, and the whatever-it-is . . ."

"Walnut tree."

"Walnut tree over there."

"Good. Now all we have to do is dig."

Kat got down on her knees and vigorously scratched leaves out of the way. If she had to paw through this soil with her bare hands she was going to find evidence that the Blue Songs had lived here.

Nathan laughed. "Cluuuck, cluck-cluck."

"Quiet. If I'm a hen, you're a big ol' gopher."

"I've got another shovel in the back of the truck."

"Can't wait that long," she said, puffing excited little breaths while she dug.

"Kat Woman, you're not going to find any—"

"I found a piece of metal!"

Nathan knelt beside her and looked. Just a few inches beneath the humus her fingers had scratched something flat and rusty. "Let me," he told her, easing her hands aside and edging the shovel under the discovery.

Kat clasped her dirty hands to her mouth and watched raptly as Nathan pried a large door hinge out of the ground.

To her it might have been a bar of gold. "A door hinge," she said in awe. "Oh, Nathan, we found their house!"

"Maybe." He brushed dirt from the corroded metal. It was spread open, the axis rusted solid. "Made of iron, I think. Handmade by a blacksmith, probably. Looks like it even might have had some fancy scroll work on it."

"That'd mean they had something nicer than a cabin?"

"Maybe."

"Look!" She scratched into the ground and held up something else. "Nails!"

Nathan took them. "Handmade." He smiled at her with an explorer's gleam of discovery in his eyes. "That'd be right for the time period, Kat. Early eighteen hundreds. I think we're on to something."

Kat whooped with glee, grasped his face between her hands, and planted a smacking kiss on his mouth. Then she drew back, laughing and pleasantly delirious. In a more deliberate spirit he slid both arms around her waist, curved himself over her possessively, and lowered his mouth on hers.

Kat felt his arms bending her, letting her drape backward as he brushed her lips gently, then took full command with a poignantly controlled tenderness that hinted at less patient intentions.

It wasn't a lingering kiss, but it was a thorough one, covering every inch of her lips, imprinting her with the complete taste and feel of him as he turned it into a series of teasing movements. Over and over he paused, lifted, almost broke contact, then pressed downward again.

Kat moaned softly and lifted her mouth to seek

more. She thought she knew how to kiss, she thought she'd been kissed well before; now she realized that Nathan Chatham had just raised her standard to a level no other man was likely to satisfy.

He lapped his tongue forward just a little and she touched hers to it wetly. With that brief, very intimate ending, like a dramatic coda for a sweet piece of music, he sat back and let go of her.

Kat saw the ruddy desire in his face and the troubled remorse in his half-shut eyes. It confused and depressed her. Why would kissing her make him feel bad?

"I always get excited when I find rusty metal," he quipped, his voice gruff.

"Sure. Me, too." Kat gestured awkwardly toward the ground. "Are you going to do that every time I find a nail?" *I'll dig faster, if that's the case.*

"Nah. You're safe." He scrubbed a hand over his face, as if making sure he hadn't lost something in the exchange.

Kat bit her lip. "I, uhmmm, I got dirt on your mouth."

He laughed hoarsely. "I didn't notice."

"Sorry."

"I *like* the taste of topsoil."

"Here, let me wipe it off." Embarrassed, Kat licked her fingers in preparation, and got dirt on her tongue. "Yaaah!" She covered her mouth and turned away from Nathan, spitting and trying to be delicate about it.

If his roaring laughter was any indication, he'd just seen the funniest sight of his life. Kat reached back and flailed at him. When she finally looked up again, wiping her mouth with the back of her hand, he was smoothing tears from the corners of his eyes.

Well, at least she'd changed the awkward, heated mood.

"Dig, gopher," she ordered, her mouth quirking with humor.

He smiled. "Scratch, hen."

By early afternoon they'd assembled a small pile of nails, three door hinges, something that looked like the handle of a cooking pot, and various pieces of iron that had been part of implements they couldn't identify.

Nathan watched Kat work and marveled at her tenacity. Her T-shirt clung to her like a wet rag—which gave him an even better reason to watch. She had sweaty streaks of grime on her arms and legs, loose strands of inky-black hair clung to her face, and her hands were covered in dirt.

But she was smiling.

He thrust his shovel into the soil and ripped out another piece of Blue Song land. The symbolism of what he was doing stabbed him with anger and frustration. The scars he made in her land today were a faint scratch compared to what he planned to do later.

Again he thrust the shovel downward, feeling disgusted and letting the aggression leap into his work. With a dull clang the blade hit something large and very solid.

"Kat!"

She limped over quickly. "What?"

They both knelt down. Nathan dug his hands into the soil and grunted with the effort of dislodging the heavy piece. "What the hell?"

"It looks like a big bar of iron."

"Not a bar—a, ummmph, rod." The thick, rusty object came loose and Nathan lifted it up. "Must be fifteen, twenty pounds."

They both looked at it curiously. The corrosion had left its surface pitted and lumpy. It was about a foot and a half long and nearly as thick as a man's wrist.

"Something to fight with?" Kat asked. "Look, there's a hanger on one end."

Nathan turned the rod upright and studied the crude eyelet forged to it. Understanding dawned quickly. "It's a window sash weight!"

Kat touched the strange device curiously. "You mean to make a window stay open when you raise it?"

"Yeah. There were two for each window—four if you wanted both halves of the window to move. Do you know what this means?"

"No." She gazed up at him with wide green eyes.

"It means the Blue Songs had a really nice house. A house with expensive glass-paned windows that only people with money could afford."

He studied the sash weight intensely. "When the Cherokees were kicked out of north Georgia there wasn't much more here than crude gold mines and one-mule farms. The Blue Songs may have owned one of the nicest places around, Cherokee or white."

Kat grabbed his arm. The yearning look in her eyes nearly tore him apart. "Do you think we could find the foundation of the house?"

Nathan nodded. *If she asked him with that child-like eagerness, he'd search for ice water in hell.* "And if we find most of these sash weights, we can get an idea of how many windows there were." He angled his head toward the forest beyond. "I bet we can even get some idea of where the outbuildings were—barns, smokehouse, stuff like that."

She sank down and gave him a teary smile. "Thank you, sweetcakes, thank you. I would never have found this place if you hadn't been here."

His heart thudding with pleasure, he told her, "We need help with this. Somebody trustworthy, some-body who won't go over to Gold Ridge and talk. The last thing we want are souvenir hunters coming out here from town."

He paused, thinking. "Got it. I'll call a friend who works for . . . with me."

She didn't notice his slip of the tongue, and she

stroked his arm with her small, gentle hand. "Nathan," she asked softly, "why are you doing all this for me?"

Because I want you to have something from this old homeplace to remember. Because I don't want you to feel so hurt later. Because I'm crazy about you.

Nathan offered her a jaunty grin. "I told you, finding rusty metal is exciting."

She was blissfully exhausted, and so happy she didn't care if she looked like a dirt dauber. Riding in the plush comfort of Nathan's truck, listening to a tape of music made by Cujimo Indians in some little South American country called Surador, she watched mountainside farms give way to the small-town charm of Gold Ridge.

What had once been a bawdy gold boomtown full of saloons, brothels, and gambling houses had become in modern times a cozy place of bed-and-breakfast inns, shops, and restaurants. There was a picturesque college campus right off a courthouse square crowded with big oak trees, and places a short walk from the main street where tourists paid five dollars an hour to pan for gold dust. Mountains rose like an exquisitely hand-painted backdrop in the distance.

"I could really be happy in a little place like this," Kat noted.

Nathan turned the tape player off and tapped the steering wheel rhythmically, thinking. "I've got a great idea. Let's get a couple of rooms at one of the inns and celebrate by staying in town tonight."

"We couldn't get service at a drive-through window, the way we look."

"We'll go shopping. We'll get the rooms and take a bath . . . baths."

Kat squirmed inwardly. She had no money for such things. "Nah."

"You shouldn't go back to the campsite today. You've already been on your bad foot too long."

"I'm okay."

"I'll pay."

"Nope."

Nathan slipped a hand under the seat and withdrew a sturdy plastic box. He handed it to her. "Open it."

Inside Kat found a half dozen major credit cards and a wad of money as big as her fist. The top bill was a fifty. Were all the others fifties?

"Nathan, is it too late for me to learn geology? I want to be rich, too."

He smiled. "Then you'll let me pay."

"No—"

"You wouldn't be out of work right now if you hadn't rescued me from Lady Savage. You're losing money, and I'm responsible. I owe ya, kid, I owe ya."

She was still staring at the money and cards. What did he do—carry his life savings around with him? Maybe it wasn't all he had, but it was undoubtedly a lot more than *her* life savings.

"Okay. But nothing fancy."

She didn't trust the mischievous sound of his laughter.

Nathan slid back into the truck with a big smile on his face. "All set. A great place. I see why you and your cousins liked it."

Kat peered around him at the Kirkland Inn, a noble old house with an upper gallery, lots of rocking chairs, and a yard filled with azaleas and dogwoods under an umbrella of stately beech trees.

"Well, we only stayed here a little while when we came to see Dove's lawyer about the will. But Tess said it has the *ambience* of an English farmhouse, and Erica said it has strong floor joists."

Nathan pursed his mouth and looked away, smiling. "You and your cousins have got to be an interesting trio."

She punched him lightly on the shoulder. "Now what?"

He cranked the truck. "Clothes."

Fifteen minutes later she stood in the aisle of a boutique, being eyed by a saleswoman who obviously thought she was an ethnic hobo of some sort. Kat went to Nathan, who sat on a wooden bench by the door, looking as happy as a clam—a dirt-covered clam in grimy buckskins, hiking boots, and a sweaty, stained T-shirt.

Kat bent over and whispered, "That walrus acts like we're scum. She's afraid I'm gonna steal something. Let's leave."

He flipped the stem of his empty pipe into his mouth and grinned rakishly around it. "Whatd'ya care? She'll jump when she sees money."

Kat frowned at him. "I hate it when salespeople look at me this way. Circus people aren't trusted, especially in little towns. I grew up with women like that making me feel like a thief."

His smile faded and he pressed her hand gently. "You know, if you'd stop checking all the price tags she might relax."

Kat lowered her voice even more. "Stuff here costs too much, Nathan."

"We're not leaving until you buy everything you need. No more looking at price tags. Hurry up. I've got to get some clean clothes too, you know. And a bath. And I'm hungry. And I want to smoke my pipe."

"All right!"

He counted on his fingers. "A dress, shoes, underwear, and whatever else females need. I want to see it all on the counter. Don't hold back."

She smiled at him with clenched teeth. "The only thing I'm holding back is my fist."

Kat felt a mixture of horror and victorious thrill

fifteen minutes later when Nathan calmly handed the saleswoman two hundred dollars plus change. With two hundred dollars Kat could have brought a whole year's wardrobe.

The woman's eyes bugged out a little and her attitude became a great deal more pleasant. Kat gripped the counter. She'd never spent that much money on one outfit before.

Well, one outfit plus underwear and small bottles of shampoo and conditioner so she could wash her hair. She should have left the hair stuff out.

"I'm sorry, Nathan," she said fervently, as they walked to the truck. "Lord, I'm so sorry. I should have looked at the prices."

"Kat, quit yowling." He tossed her shopping bags into the back of the truck. "It's all right."

"No, it's not. It's not right for you to spend this much money."

"Think I expect something in return?" he asked coolly, one dark brow arched in warning.

"If you do, I sure feel obligated!"

The color drained out of his face. "I didn't realize that you trade sex for clothes. I should have bought you more."

She shook her head angrily. "You know what I mean!"

He gripped her shoulders hard and looked down at her with eyes gone the cold pewter color that meant he was angry. He said softly, "If I want anything from you, I'll just ask. I won't bribe you for it."

She was so flustered that she almost said, *So ask.* Kat nodded numbly. "Sorry. I'm not used to gentlemen."

"Well, *get* used."

I'd love to, Nathan. Especially a gentleman with a cute tattooed behind and a sexy pierced ear. Kat limped to her side of the truck but didn't get a chance to touch the door. Nathan leapt in front of her, pulled it open, and bowed, his expression droll but still a little angry.

"Hah," she said imperiously, and got inside.

She had a lovely room full of antiques. It opened on to the inn's back gallery, and when she walked to the railing she could touch the limb of a beech tree close by.

The beech tree was the only thing close by. Nathan had asked for a room on the other side of the house.

Why did he make it clear that he liked her, wanted her as a woman, but intended to avoid her? Kat stood in the shower and scrubbed her hair fiercely, trying to wash him out of it, as the old song said.

Okay, so she was a nobody, a nomad with no immediate future outside of the weird show biz world of wrestling. She wasn't cut out to get an ordinary job. It would drive her nuts, seeing the same office or store every day, sitting still most of the time.

Nathan had a good job, not a normal job, but an entirely respectable, even sort of glamorous one. He had money. He certainly had no trouble attracting women—she'd watched a salesgirl nearly drool over him in the men's store a little while ago. And he was really sophisticated, despite what he said about having only one year of college.

Nathan even had a regular family back in Arkansas and had grown up on the homeplace Nathaniel Chatham had acquired before the Civil War. He had *roots.*

In short, Nathan didn't need a female wrestler with no education, no decent clothes, a credit rating that made loan officers laugh, and a personal history that included rape plus a failed marriage.

She could just imagine how his family would freak if he brought home an almost full-blooded Injun who was also a Gallatin. They'd be conjuring up General Custer inside of twenty-four hours.

Nathan liked her, he was her friend, and he even

wanted to make love to her. But he wasn't going to do it, because he was a gentleman, and he knew she'd be hurt when he left.

And on that point he was very, very right.

Nathan stood on the back balcony, waiting anxiously. He hadn't seen her in an hour. He rocked in a rocking chair. He walked. He held a conversation with a *salali* gathering green acorns on one of the trees and a tabby *wis-sah* that wanted to gather the *salali.*

Finally he shoved his hands through his hair and muttered oaths which made both the *salali* and the *wis-sah* run away. Would this get worse? Would he get to the point where he couldn't stand to be away from her for thirty minutes, then fifteen, then five, until eventually he'd become her constant shadow?

At the other end of the gallery her door opened. Nathan glanced at his scrubbed hiking boots, brushed a tiny piece of tobacco off the tan trousers he'd purchased, fiddled with his suspenders, and checked the rolled-up sleeves of a striped shirt that still smelled like a menswear shop despite all the pipe smoke he'd blown on it.

God, he hadn't been this antsy the night he'd had to explain to a Zambinawee chief that he didn't want to get married, even if it meant he'd own all four of the chief's daughters.

Kat stepped onto the gallery, fluffing her hair as if it weren't quite dry. Nathan gripped the gallery railing and stared at her.

She'd chosen a white dress of some crinkly white material. The short-sleeved bodice knew what to do over her curves and the full skirt knew how to swirl gracefully around her legs.

The white material heightened the honey of her skin and made her hair look blue-black. The dress's neckline was decorated with white fringe and brightly colored beads, giving it a boutique-Indian look that would have been too cute on anyone but a real Indian. With the dress she wore plain white sandals and absolutely no jewelry or makeup. Regardless, she looked exotic.

Nathan wanted to eat her alive. In Cherokee love formulas, that was the ultimate compliment.

She saw him and abruptly stopped stroking her hair. Her hands framed her face, making a lovely picture which imprinted itself forever in Nathan's mind.

Kat lowered her arms, tilted her head to one side, looked him up and down with unmistakable distress, then quickly adjusted her expression and smiled widely.

"Hi ya, sweetcakes."

She was still edgy around him, he realized, and she wasn't going to take him seriously, no matter how much money he had. *It was time to do a little work on the hair.*

Nathan walked toward her calmly, putting what he hoped was a cocky smile on his face. "That outfit's great, Katlanicha."

"Two hundred bucks' worth?"

"Two thousand."

"That's what my car cost."

He reached her and halted, noting the darkening of her cheeks. Her complexion didn't show a blush, but it took on a richer color, as if someone were mixing strawberries with the honey.

Her eyes flickered with tension but held his gaze. "Ready for dinner?"

"Is your hair dry?" he said softly.

"Oh, yeah . . ."

Nathan slid his hands into it, lifted it on both sides, and studied it as if truly concerned about dryness. "A little damp. Sit down and let me air it for you."

He took one look at her sloe-eyed expression and

knew he'd scored a direct hit. "Sure," she squeaked, then cleared her throat and said, "*Sure.*"

She went to a cushioned bench by the gallery railing and sat down stiffly, tucking her skirt around her in a defensive way.

"Lean forward," Nathan crooned. "Lean on the railing."

Slowly, glancing over her shoulder with doleful wariness which reminded him of a worried puppy, she rested her forearms on the rail. Finally she faced forward and lowered her chin on her hands.

The mane of hair flowed down her back like a beautiful black river. Nathan didn't think he had a hair fetish, but his body reacted that way.

He stroked his fingers through her hair, gathered it in one hand, then put the other hand underneath, palm up, at the base of her head. Nathan wove his fingers up into the black silk and pulled them along the underside, letting strands slip free until he was holding only a single lock when he reached the end.

Tugging it playfully, he brushed the feathery tip along one of her arms.

Kat trembled. "I don't think you're *airing,* I think you're *daring,*" she murmured hoarsely. "And it's not funny, okay?"

Nathan dropped the strand of hair, smoothed it into place, and silently cursed himself for pushing her too far, too soon. "I was just teasing," he assured her. "Relax."

"Just teasing." She lifted her head, brushed a hand across her eyes, and sighed. "Jeez, I'm tired and crabby. Sure you want to go to dinner with me?"

"We'll be tired and crabby together. Come on."

When she turned to look up at him her eyes seemed ancient and sad and familiar in a way that made him feel desperate.

"Aw, Katie," he whispered, the nickname coming

to his lips so easily. "I've been waiting a long time, too."

She erased her strange expression, stood up, and patted his shoulder like a pal. "Yeah, I made you wait while I primped. You must be starving for some dinner. Let's go. We can cut through my room to the hall."

Smiling crookedly, she breezed past him and into the house. Nathan frowned in bewilderment. He wasn't certain what he'd been talking about, but he knew it had nothing to do with dinner.

Nathan kept brooding about his strange words, and he was still puzzling over them as he lay in bed that night. The inn's wide, soft four-poster was hard on his back, accustomed as he was to sleeping on the ground. So sleep eluded him.

Lost in deep thought, he lifted a hand to a streak of moonlight on his coverlet. Some things were eternal—moonlight, sunlight, souls. He couldn't shake the feeling that there was more between him and Kat than their brief relationship warranted.

There'd been no shortage of women in his life; he'd broken hearts and had his broken in return, more than once. But he'd never felt anything like this before. Was it just a special brand of man-woman chemistry, wonderful but nothing mysterious? If so, then why did he keep saying things to her that he didn't understand, as if they'd been buried inside him long before he met her, just waiting to be said to her alone?

Listen, O Ancient White Fire! This woman's soul has come to rest with me, and I will never let it go.

Nathan was a very spiritual man, and he believed many things were possible. But as much as he was drawn to Kat, he wasn't certain he believed that he'd known her before.

He groaned in dismay, laughed wearily, and sat

up in bed, holding his head in both hands. If he'd been through this torment in another life, he damned sure wouldn't have forgotten it. Nathan cursed in jovial disgust and got up, pulling the bedcovers with him. He'd sleep on the floor and pretend he'd once been a rug.

As he dropped the covers his ears picked up the sound of hurrying feet. Listening intently, Nathan gazed at he door that led from his room on to the gallery.

It was glass-paned and curtained with diaphanous white material that let him immediately identify the small, shadowy form that halted there. He had the door open before Kat knocked.

"What's the matter?" he asked quickly.

She stood there half-hidden in moonlight, barefoot, still wearing her new dress because it was the only clean clothing she had. In one hand she held a book of local history they'd bought at a store on the town square.

"I'm sorry, I had to talk to you," she said in a tear-soaked voice.

"Katie, what is it?" He drew her inside and shut the door.

She held the book up, her hand trembling. "My great-great-grandfather Justis never married Katlanicha. He couldn't have. He had a white wife and family here."

Six

Nathan went to a bedside table and fumbled with the switch on an old-fashioned globe lamp. When he finally had it working he pivoted to find Kat wiping her eyes and trying desperately to look calm.

"Katie," he whispered sadly, and went to her with his arms held out. "It couldn't be that bad."

She leaned against him, her face burrowed into his shoulder, and he held her snugly, stroking her disheveled hair.

"I was in bed reading this d-damned book," she said, her chest rising and falling in a shallow, swift rhythm. "I had to come tell you about it."

The book was entitled *Gold Ridge—The Early Years. A Newspaper History.* It contained the complete texts of the town's first paper, a crudely typeset weekly called the *Gold Ridge Gazette.*

Nathan took the thick hardcover and tossed it on the floor, then hugged her sympathetically. "What'd you find, gal?"

"Well, the paper started about three years before the Cherokees left, 'cause it talks about how Gold Ridge was being built on land owned by the Cherokee Nation but how that was okay 'cause the govern-

To get a free *Loveswept* ® calendar, packed with information about *Loveswept* romances in 1990, simply fill out the form below.

*C*alendar available early December, 1989. Offer good while supplies last.

Name _____

Address _____

City _____ State_____ Zip _____

Would you please give us the following information:

Did you buy Loveswept Golden Classics (on sale in June)?
____Yes ____No

If your answer is yes, did you buy __1 __2 __3 __4

Will you buy Golden Classics featuring Hometown Hunks on the covers?
I will buy 1-2____, 3-4 ____, All 6____ None____

How often would you like to have an opportunity to purchase Golden Classics?
Every month_____ If so, how many per month_____
Quarterly_____

* One calendar per household.

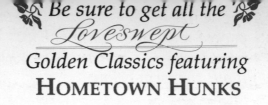

Be sure to get all the *Loveswept*
Golden Classics featuring
HOMETOWN HUNKS

On sale in October

BUSINESS REPLY MAIL

FIRST-CLASS MAIL   PERMIT NO. 174   NEW YORK, NY

Postage will be paid by addressee

Loveswept

Bantam Books
Dept. CN
666 Fifth Avenue
New York, NY 10103

ment was negotiating a treaty to make the Indians leave."

Nathan kept caressing her hair and hoped she wouldn't notice that he was wearing nothing but white briefs. He didn't want her to move away.

He didn't have to worry. She put her free arm around his bare waist and held him as if he were a life buoy in a stormy sea.

"Justis must have been a VIP around here," she continued. "There was a list of big mines, and two of 'em were owned by the Gallatin Company. There was a Gallatin General Store, and a Gallatin Hotel, and even a Gallatin saloon."

She tilted her head back and looked at Nathan wretchedly. "Justis was a gold miner. He came here to take gold out of Cherokee land, just like all the other settlers. I bet he was only interested in Katlanicha because he thought there was gold on her family's farm."

Nathan kissed her forehead and tried to ignore the ugly pang of guilt about his own intentions. "There's too much we'll never know. It could've been different from how it sounds. I mean, if all he wanted was gold, then he didn't have to stay with her out in Oklahoma and raise children with her, right?"

New tears slid over Kat's black lashes. "I was givin' him the benefit of the doubt until I came to the m-marriage part. The year after the Cherokees got kicked out, the year after great-great-grandmother and her family had to leave"—she exhaled raggedly—"Justis married a judge's daughter named Amarintha Parnell."

Her voice became bitter. "The judge was a VIP too. He owned a mine here. I guess Justis wanted to have a proper wife from a real good *white* family."

Nathan felt so bad for her that he hardly knew what to say. "But ol' Justis didn't stay with Amarintha. You *know* that." He tried to joke. "He couldn't have loved some babe with a prissy little name like Amarintha."

Kat laughed sharply. "Well, he might not have loved her, but he sure did sleep with her a time or two, 'cause six months later the paper ran a birth announcement. Her and Justis had a baby girl."

Nathan made an inarticulate sound of distress and then a soothing one. "It's all right. Sssh. He must have divorced her later and married your great-great-grandmother."

"Divorce? Back then? No." She jabbed a finger toward the offending book. "The society column mentions four or five times *during the next fifteen years* when he came back to Gold Ridge to take care of his businesses and visit his wife. Course, the paper makes it sound respectable—like there's nothing strange about a husband and wife not living together all the time."

She sighed. "Then Amarintha and the daughter died from some sort of fever that was going around. The paper listed their names in the obituaries."

"Well, let's see," Nathan said hopefully. "Fifteen years later, that'd be 1853. Hmmm, Justis could have married Katlanicha *then*."

"Yeah, after they already had three sons."

"Who says they did? I only know about Holt, and he was just a kid during the Civil War. He could have been born in 1853."

Kat patted his cheek in gratitude. "Harmonica man, you're playing a happy tune, but it's not workin'. Erica's and Tess's great-grandpas were old enough to fight in the Civil War. Erica says hers was shot as a spy—and he was old enough to leave behind a wife and a son."

She shook her head. "So ol' Justis had himself two families going at the same time—one nice and legal and white, the other one . . . the other one . . ."

Nathan ached with sorrow as she looked up at him in anguish. "Oh, Nathan, great-great-grandmother was just his *Indian* wife, and back then that meant she wasn't anything." Her face crinkled with the effort of holding back more tears. "People didn't just think of my great-grandpa Holt as a killer, they thought of him as a bastard."

Nathan swallowed a lump in his throat as she clung to him, crying softly. "Kat, don't set so much store by niceties. A lot of men—white and Cherokee—had more than one wife. Some Cherokee women had more than one husband, or several husbands one right after the other.

"Things weren't real legal and neat, and nobody cared. Most likely nobody thought anything about Justis and Katlanicha's arrangement. They were probably married in a Cherokee ceremony. That's just as good."

"But he used her," Kat insisted. "He didn't make her a legal wife under white law, under *his* law." She clenched her hands against Nathan's chest. "And I bet I know why he stayed with her.

"I read in one of my other books that out in the Indian Territory a white man could claim Cherokee land if he had a Cherokee wife."

Nathan grimaced. She was right on that point. "Yeah, that's the way it was. And here in Georgia, too, when this town was still part of the Cherokee Nation."

She made a hoarse sound of disgust. "Justis had the best of both worlds—a respectable white wife and a profitable Indian one."

"It doesn't matter."

"Yes, it does!" Her green eyes—eyes inherited from Justis—glittered with anger. "You don't know what it's like to want *so much* to have something to be proud of. I do! You wanna know why I never talk about my mother? She was from the reservation up in North Carolina. *Her* people sold moonshine and stole cars!"

"So who cares?"

"I care!" She began to thump his chest for emphasis. "Growing up, I was snubbed by regular people who figure circus performers are scum, and now I'm snubbed by people who think lady wrestlers are tramps! And, hey, I'm a multiminority representative when it comes to getting insulted by confused bigots! Name your choice—I'm not only Indian, I'm Cuban, Mexican, Oriental, and Iranian—and once some jerk even called me a 'whale-sucking Eskimo'!"

"Kat, you're denting my rib cage. Calm down."

She grasped his face between her hands and searched his eyes for answers, for help. "Is it too much to want respect and love just for *me*, for what I am, no matter how different I am from everybody else?" Her voice was low and choked. "I don't want to go through the rest of my life bein' raped and used and laughed at."

Nathan inhaled sharply. Oh God, she hurt so much. "Katie, I'll make it up to you, I swear," he said hoarsely, caught in a blinding need to right every wrong that had ever been done to her. "We can have it *all* this time."

"*This* time?"

Nathan shut his eyes and grimaced. "I don't know what I'm saying, but I know what I mean." She was stroking his face with quick, possessive little caresses, her hands trembling.

"Katie," he said again, without thinking. *That nickname was part of his soul.* Nathan shuddered with emotion. "Forget what you read tonight. Trust me."

That was stranger than what he'd already said. Nathan looked at her anxiously. "I don't make sense around you. I want you too much to make sense. Don't run scared because I'm this way."

She moaned softly. "I'm not scared. I haven't been scared since the first time you called me 'Katie.' Oh, Nathan, what's going on between us?"

"I don't understand it either," he whispered, lifting her onto her toes. His voice dropped even lower. "I don't have to understand it."

She slid her arms around his neck. "Make love to me," she begged. "I won't ask for too much."

"You won't have to ask. Everything—everything you want, or need—it's yours."

"You, I need you," she cried as he covered her mouth with his.

They were quick, almost rough, fired by needs and emotions that swept the whole world away to leave only the two of them touching, loving, seeking to give pleasure.

Her dress barely survived. Nathan no sooner jerked the bodice open in back than she was fiercely struggling to get her arms out of it. Underneath she wore absolutely nothing. He pulled the dress down to her waist and she tugged him to her, her eyes flaring when her naked breasts flattened against his chest. He reached between their bodies to squeeze her nipples, pulling them forward, rubbing the peaks, wrapping his fingers around first one breast and then the other in an almost frantic desire to make her back arch again and again.

The dress fell off her hips, leaving only one barrier between them. Nathan thought he would burn up from the pure, lovely bawdiness in her as she slid her hands under the waistband of his briefs.

"I couldn't walk away when I saw you taking a bath that day," she told him. "I never saw a man enjoy being naked so much. I wanted to be naked with you."

"Now you are." His briefs fell to his ankles and he stepped out of them.

Immediately he curved both hands down her spine, underneath the mane of hair, along the curve of her rump, then beneath it, so that he could pull her to his hardness.

She gasped with delight as the ridge nestled into her belly, and he thought there would never be a more exquisite sensation in his life than the feel of her soft mound fitted to the tops of his thighs.

"Nice," she whispered. "And remember, I'm not real good with words."

"You're great with body language."

He picked her up. Her thighs wrapped around his waist and her arms circled his neck in a deep embrace. With his face near enough for her mobile, sweet little mouth to enjoy, she kissed whatever she could reach, from earring to mustache and everything else.

Nathan staggered from sensation, dimly aware that he was flexing against her and that she was answering the primitive, erotic invitation with movements of her own. She dug the necklace from between them and kissed the nugget.

"I want to kiss everything on you and everything that ever touched you," she explained.

Nathan heard the breath slide from his mouth in a sigh of helpless surrender. The spontaneous movements of their bodies joined them suddenly. Kat made a high-pitched keening sound and, panting, looked at him through half-shut eyes.

He knew from her silkiness that he hadn't hurt her. He had surprised her, though.

"You're so strong," she murmured breathlessly, and the devotion in her eyes told him that she loved his surprise.

"I can hold you," he promised, and squeezed his hands into her thighs to lift her a little higher on his body.

"Hold me," she begged, kissing him deeply, slipping her tongue in and out of his mouth and filling him with a hunger that poured extraordinary strength into him.

She was no heavier than a dream, and he moved inside her easily, nuzzling his face along her shoulder, kissing her, biting her, licking her throat when her head fell back and she cried out to him.

Nathan's knees buckled a little at the feel of her pulsing with release. Her wail of pleasure held surprise and fierce happiness.

He found himself laughing and almost crying and on the verge of filling her with everything he could give. "It's like this with you and me, Katie," he shouted with delight. "Didn't you always know it would be like this?"

Her head fell forward and she sank her mouth onto his for a long moment, which brought him into a realm he'd never known before. "*Yes*," she said against his mouth. "Always."

Nathan dropped to his knees and arched into her in one final, explosive moment that made his head sag back even as his fingers dug into her and she gave him more—more of her body, more of her fire, more of her soul.

They collapsed onto the floor together, her on top of him, still joined, their skin slick with sweat, their breaths mingling in a turbulent search for the center of the storm.

All Nathan could manage to do was nuzzle her face and hold onto her with the same exhausted grip she had on him. "Now, Katie," he whispered, "we can start again."

Whatever he meant, she stroked his face and hair and smiled down at him with joyful tears in her eyes. "I know."

She had to learn everything about him, everything that those handsome, droopy eyes had seen and everything that weathered, work-hardened body had done, everything that had made him into the man she now loved.

Nathan protested that he felt like her private playground, but the smile he gave her said that he didn't mind a bit. She made him lie on the bed while she nuzzled her face over his torso, licking and kissing the sweaty, sexy essence until he swore she was trying to eat him alive.

Kat lifted his hands to study the scars and calluses from rough work and dangerous encounters. She traced the lines in his palms, thinking how his past and future seemed to merge with the blemishes; this man had never avoided a challenge, and it showed in his hands.

Now he'd brought that challenge into her life, and she would read his body like a map, trying to understand him so well that she could find his heart, and keep it.

Kat stroked a fingertip over the fine white lines on his right knuckles. "You used to fight?"

"Just enough to keep my hide in one piece so you'd enjoy it one day." Oh, he knew how to make an electric jolt of pleasure slide through her, and he recognized it in her eyes. "I like your hide, too," he promised softly, brushing his scarred knuckle over his breasts and smiling when the peaks grew harder.

"You're plain *wicked*, Nathan Chatham." She arched one black brow at him. "You ever fight over a woman?"

"Yep." He waited just long enough for her to thump his chest in exasperation. "I punched a water buffalo that was about to do a tap dance on an old Australian lady."

"Oh." She took his hand again and kissed the knuckles. "Other fights?"

"I had a run-in with some local boys down in Surador last year. Just helping out an acquaintance of mine."

When Kat looked at him quizzically he explained, "Fellow I met while I was studying some sites. Said he was an anthropologist, but I suspect he was in some sort of government work. Nice guy, but a funny name—Surprise. Kyle Surprise. He hung around with me for a few weeks, then moved on.

"I heard later that he'd gotten into some trouble.

One of the nationalist *patróns* didn't like Kyle's brand of anthropology, I think. Had him locked up on a banana plantation." Nathan shrugged. "I just organized a few of the rebel troops and got him out."

Pride swept over Kat, making her bend forward quickly and kiss him. "You're a wonder."

"Wonder all right. Wonder what you're gonna do to me next."

She sat back, stroked the hard plane of his belly, and said in a husky tone, "I'm gonna turn you over and see that tattoo. I want to know all about it."

"Got it on the Amazon."

"That's not where *I* saw it."

Chuckling, he rolled onto his stomach without the least hint of shyness and propped his chin on crossed arms.

Kat smiled in delight. "It looks like a clown face!"

Nathan huffed loudly. "That's Numanchuko, the god of earth. The natives said Numanchuko must like me if he let me know his secrets."

"Secrets?"

"Gold."

"Oh." Kat molded her hands to Nathan's back and drew them down to his thighs, watching the muscles flex in response. "Numanchuko's lively," she noted.

"I think he expects an earthquake."

"I expect he's right. I'm gonna get real friendly with him."

Wanting to be close to Nathan in ways she'd never wanted with any other man, she draped herself on top of him like a blanket, smiling a little at the thought of the colorful tattoo face flattened under her stomach.

"Ol' Numanchuko's never had it so good," Nathan said with a soft groan.

Kat nibbled the back of his neck, stroked a small patch of hair between his shoulder blades, then slowly slid her hands down his sides.

"Nathan? I want another pony ride."

He slipped a hand into her hair and guided her upward so that her head was next to his. Kat curled over him, giggling when their mouths met awkwardly, losing the breath to giggle when he rebuked her with a deliciously rough tongue. She moved and lay in his arms, pulled chest to chest with him, her thighs hugging the leg he angled between them.

He drew her lower lip between his teeth, nibbled it, then let go slowly and licked the swollen skin like a wild animal tasting his mate. Kat shut her eyes and still saw him, imagined the primal glitter in his eyes, the ruffled hair of his desperado mustache a little damp from the wet kiss they'd just shared.

"Kat, does the pony need a saddle?"

Tenderness sleeted through her when she understood his hint. Kat laughed helplessly. "Nope."

He held her closer and nuzzled his crooked nose to her slightly dished one. "Just want to protect you. I wish I could say I thought about it before, but I was only thinking that I'd die if I didn't get inside you. That's not like me—to be so desperate that I forget. I swear."

She crooned a reassuring sound. "I like the compliment." Kat hesitated a moment, then told him, "I got an IUD not too long before . . . before that guy left."

"That guy?"

"I don't want to call him 'my husband.' " She watched her forefinger swirl ringlets into Nathan's damp chest hair. "I don't want to do him the honor anymore."

Abruptly Nathan's hand was behind her head, bringing her to his mouth, holding her while he kissed her for a long, infinitely sweet time. "You got the right idea," he whispered eventually. "Forget you ever knew him. Forget anybody ever touched you but me."

She heard her own shallow breath and absorbed

the giving, mobile pressure of his hand as he slid it between her thighs. "Nobody ever has," Kat promised.

As he rose over her she locked her gaze on his face, trying to see inside him, hoping she could pour all of her love into him until he had no choice but to love her back.

He cared for the earth, wore its offering on his body, took from it as her great-great-grandfather had done, but Nathan had honesty and honor; he gave respect in return. On her land, her ancestors' land, she and Nathan had formed a very special bond that went beyond explanation.

And she believed that the land would keep them together.

Late the next morning—it was closer to afternoon when they left Nathan's room—they went downstairs to the inn's office.

While Nathan called Tri-State on a phone at the manager's desk, Kat used one in the main hall. Erica had no phone at Dove Gallatin's house in North Carolina, so she'd given Kat the number at the Tall Wolf home.

"*Osiyo*," a hearty male voice answered.

Kat searched the mental catalogue of Cherokee terms Nathan had taught her. It was a small catalogue at this point. Ah. Hello. "*Osiyo*. Is this Grandpa Sam?"

"Yeah! Who's this?"

"Kat Gallatin, Erica's cousin."

"The *wah lay lee*. Sure!"

"Erica told me your family would take messages for her."

"Sure! Shoot!"

"Tell her she can get in touch with me by calling Drake Lancaster at the Kirkland Inn." Kat relayed the inn's phone number while Grandpa Sam took it down slowly. "Tell her Drake will be here next week. He works for the mining company. He's a . . ." She paused, thinking. For the sake of brevity she wouldn't explain who Nathan was and that Drake Lancaster was a friend and fellow employee for Tri-State. "Drake's a good friend of mine," Kat finished.

"Got it, *wah lay lee*."

Kat wished she could talk directly with Erica. She needed to share the disturbing information about Justis Gallatin's white wife and hear Erica's opinion. But for now she could only struggle to remember the word for "thank you" in Cherokee. Ah.

"*Wado*, Grandpa Sam."

He hooted with pleasure. "Somebody's teachin' you to be an Indian!"

Kat smiled broadly as she hung up the phone. Somebody was teaching her how to feel fantastic.

Suddenly two strong hands circled her waist from behind. Kat looked down at their tanned contrast against her white dress, the lean, callused fingers digging into the material with delicious possession. A mustache brushed her right ear.

"Ma'am, I'm a stranger to these parts—"

"Not *those* parts—"

"And I been staring at you from the manager's desk," Nathan whispered in a throaty, seductive voice. "You're the most beautiful woman I've ever seen, and I'd be tickled silly if you'd have a late breakfast with me."

Trembling as if it had been years instead of a few minutes since she'd lain in his arms, Kat glanced around to make sure no one was watching or listening, then turned her face toward that voice, that thick mustache, and the provocative masculine scent that was still on her and inside her.

"Hmmm. Well, let me tell you something, stranger, I've been awake most of the night, and I need a pot of coffee as fast as I can get it. Give me coffee and I'm yours."

"You want it strong and hot?"

"Oh yes. That's the way I'm used to it." Kat nearly dissolved into breathless laughter. "And I like my coffee that way, too."

Nathan laughed very softly against her ear, the sound a rumbling invitation to be bad. His fingers rubbed the tops of her hips, squeezing into her rhythmically. Kat's knees went weak. This wonderful man wanted her as much as she wanted him, at least in bed. She looked forward to the days ahead with gleeful enthusiasm because each minute would be spent in Nathan's company.

"Well, ma'am, what'd you do all night?" he asked, touching his lips to her earlobe.

Her breath became a sigh. "I made love in about every way a man and woman can think of."

"Oh, I bet you missed a way or two"—Nathan dropped a nibbling kiss on her neck, and she heard him inhale deeply—"but there's a sexy, sleepy look in your eyes that says you got plenty of satisfaction."

"Boy, did I. And I think my lover did, too. You wanna know what he said right around dawn?"

"Hmmm?"

"He said he felt like grinning from his tattoo to his eyebrows."

"Ma'am, I *believe* that sayin' is 'Grinning from his—' "

"Well, the tattoo's in that particular area."

"Oh."

He trailed kisses down her neck and gently sucked the spot where it joined her shoulder. Kat whimpered. A housekeeper walked out of the manager's office and did a quick double take.

"Well, excuse *me*," she said primly, and went back in again.

Kat pivoted toward Nathan and grasped his shirtfront. He bit his lip to keep from laughing. "I oughta put a wrestling hold on you," she threatened in exasperation.

"You better get me back to the woods. I don't know how much longer I can control myself."

"Oh." She feigned distress. "You're gonna control yourself?"

His sly, sideways look said that was the last thing he had in mind.

Colluvial deposits. Bull quartz. Auriferous. Intergranular. Nathan was teaching her *two* languages—Cherokee and gold mining. Both were tough.

"Colluvium, thin," he said into the small tape recorder in his hand, while his sharp gray eyes studied the rocky hillside. "Contains quartz pebbles, some cobbles, a few boulders no larger than three feet in diameter. Bedrock probably saprolitic. Underlying the area, garnetiferous mica schist. Potential auriferous veins to the southeast."

He snapped the recorder off, reached for the satellite map and a smaller topographical map which Kat held, and scribbled notes on each of them.

Then he looked up at her and smiled. "How's the ankle, Kat Woman?"

She nodded. "Fine."

"What's the matter? You look worried."

"I just keep thinking how smart you are. I feel dumb."

"Because I can reel off all those hundred-dollar words?"

"Yeah."

"They sound complicated, but they're not. I just basically said that this land has good gold-bearing potential."

Kat glanced around at majestic hardwoods, the thick greenery that surrounded them with darkly cool beauty, and the blue mountains in the distance. Unless Tri-State could disturb only a small section of land and leave the rest alone, she was against a mining lease.

"Nathan, how would Tri-State get the gold outta here? Would they dig a mine shaft, or what?"

He gently shooed something away from her hair. "Go away, grandmother *tagu*." His fingers caressed her scalp as he tucked a loose strand of hair back into her braid.

Kat's stomach dropped pleasantly and she smiled, watching the fat june bug flutter into the sunshine. "*Tagu*," she echoed.

Nathan lifted her chin with a forefinger, leaned over, and gave her a lingering kiss. "Come on," he murmured. "Let's go back to the stream. You can soak your foot and I'll show you how to pan for gold."

"Great!"

Later she remembered her question about Tri-State's mining techniques, but by then she was naked and so was Nathan, and they lay in the stream gleefully dumping handfuls of sand on each other's stomachs so that they could inspect it for gold particles.

The question no longer seemed important. Nathan would never suggest anything that would hurt her land. She was sure of it.

"*Uwodo*," he whispered into her ear.

He had his back propped against a tree. She had her back propped against his chest. His legs were around her, his big, knotty feet sliding up and down her shins. Her feet were dangling in the stream.

And his hands, oh, his hands . . .

"*Uwodo*," she repeated lazily, as he stroked her breasts with the backs of his fingers. "What's it mean?" This was a great way to learn Cherokee.

"Pretty," he answered. And then he chuckled, his breath warm on her neck. "Pretty *ganuhdi-i*."

"I guess I know what *that* means." Kat shifted her

hips inside the harbor of his thighs. "What's that I feel?"

"A worn-out *wautoli*."

They both laughed. "I like it anyhow," she assured him.

He nuzzled his face into her neck and sighed with contentment. "How's your ankle?"

She lifted it from the water. "Real good. I like your form of doctoring. Lots of rest, with plenty of company. It's working. Even when my ankle hurts, I don't notice."

"You'll go back on the tour right away?"

"Have to. Got bills to pay."

"Nope."

Kat turned her head toward his and kissed him gently. "Yep."

"Nope. I already paid 'em."

She twisted quickly and looked him straight in the eyes. "When?"

"When we were in town eating lunch the other day. You went to the ladies' room, and I made a phone call. Just told a friend of mine what to take care of."

Nathan tried to look innocent. "Just your apartment rent and utilities." When she continued to look at him speechlessly, he added, "I did it so you could stay here longer with me. Is that so bad?"

"How long are you gonna stay?" she asked.

"I don't know."

"Where will you go after you leave?"

"Surador. I've got work to do down there." He cupped her face with one hand and gazed at her tenderly. "See, Kat? We're both nomads. But even nomads can find ways to be together. I'll be back. I'll find you."

Suddenly the future was a lot less happy. Kat slid her arms around him and rested her head on his shoulder. "I'll miss you," she whispered.

"I'm not gone yet," he said gruffly, and stroked her hair.

It feels like you are, Kat told him silently.

Kat carried an armload of kindling back toward camp, barely limping now that she'd had several more days of Nathan's rather untraditional—but highly enjoyable—form of doctoring.

Sunset made long shadows hang from the trees, and bats darted across patches of sky overhead. She thought about all the Cherokee legends Nathan had told her of monsters and giants, elves and witches.

Kat chanted under her breath. "Lions and tigers and bears, oh my! Lions and tigers and bears, oh—"

"Hello," a bass voice said politely.

Kat dropped her kindling. Her heart jamming her throat, she swung around on the trail and faced an incredible sight. Oh Lord, Nathan was right. There *were* giants.

He didn't look Cherokee, but he could have been birthed by some Cherokee mountain. He stood there watching her, his neatly cropped black hair brushing a tree limb easily seven feet from the ground. He had shoulders a bodybuilder would die for, but otherwise he was streamlined. Big as a freight train, but streamlined, with a handsome, somewhat angular face.

Kat exhaled a little. No mythical giant would be dressed in a blue T-shirt, khaki trousers, and hiking boots. But she didn't like the fact that he had a knife the size of a small sword lashed into a leather scabbard on one side of his belt.

Kat backed away slowly, her hands balled into fists.

The giant's eyebrows shot up. "Wait."

"I'm little, but I'm tough," she warned in a low, fierce voice. "And I'll take a prize or two before you squash me."

He stepped forward, holding up both huge hands in a placating gesture. "I'm—"

"Dead meat," she interjected, and whipped out the Beretta that had been hidden in the front waistband of her shorts, under her floppy T-shirt. Kat pointed the gun at the center of his chest.

"Facedown on the ground. Spread-eagle. Say a word and I'll turn you into cheddar cheese . . . Swiss cheese."

Kat grimaced. She was so intimidating. She couldn't even get her cheeses right.

The giant shrugged, sighed, and lowered himself with surprising grace to the forest floor.

"Eat the ground," she ordered, feeling desperate with fear. He sighed again and stuck his face into dark humus that was damp from an afternoon rain.

"Yo, Kat!" Nathan called from somewhere in the woods near camp. He sang coyly, "Here, kitty, here, kitty!"

"Naaaathaan!" she screamed. Within seconds she heard him crashing through the forest, taking a shortcut to the trail.

He burst onto it, his hand wrapped around the hilt of his bowie knife. "What?"

"I caught this guy on our land!" *Our* seemed appropriate. It had just popped out.

Nathan ran up to her, halted in midstride, and stared at the captive, who still had his face buried in the forest floor.

Kat watched in consternation as Nathan dropped the knife, clasped his stomach, and bent over laughing. "D-Drake L-Lancaster." He wheezed. "Caught by my Katie."

Oh no. Drake Lancaster, Nathan's co-worker? She stared at the huge man in horrified embarrassment. He remained flat, but his back quivered with laughter, and he raised his head slowly. Bits of dirt and decomposed leaves were plastered to his droll expression.

"She's perfect for you, Nathan."

Drake returned from his room in Gold Ridge early the next morning, met them at the site of the Blue Song home, and squinted at Kat in amusement when she solemnly apologized one more time.

Then he stripped down to hiking shorts and boots, grabbed a shovel, and attacked the house site like a human bulldozer. Nathan wore only jogging shorts and his hiking boots, and Kat felt positively overdressed because she had to wear a bra and T-shirt with her shorts.

But after Drake returned to the inn for the day . . .

She followed the two men, picking up the things they unearthed, smiling when Nathan looked over and made clucking noises at her.

She really did feel like a little hen searching for goodies, and she found plenty to cluck about. By noon she'd stacked twenty window sash weights in a neat pyramid beside a smaller pile of nails, hinges, and miscellaneous metal.

But her big find was four buttons and a handful of musket balls.

"Nathan!" She went over to him excitedly and presented the items in her cupped palms. "Look! They were all in the same spot!"

After carefully scratching dirt off one button with a twig, Nathan's expression became pensive. He held it so that a stripe of sunlight would illuminate the features.

"It's got a U.S. Army insignia."

She frowned. "But what would that be doing near the musket balls? Nathan, are you saying a soldier was killed here? But there's no skeleton!"

Drake came over and examined the items. He was a very quiet, private person, Kat had already noticed, and he seemed to feel awkward around her, though he certainly wasn't shy. She judged he was just self-conscious in the manner of large, brutal-looking men who were accustomed to being feared whether they warranted it or not.

As he volunteered technical information about the musket balls, Kat eyed him curiously. Nathan had said that he coordinated on-site security for Tri-State mines, and it was obvious he was a weapons expert.

"So what you're saying," Nathan observed when he'd finished describing the balls, "is that these probably hit hard objects—stone or metal—not people."

"Yes. If the buttons fit the time period when the Cherokees were removed, then it's possible the army was up here, and these could be musket shots they fired inside the house."

Kat gave Nathan a troubled look. He heart felt like a small, hard fist in her chest. "Damn," she said softly.

He laid a hand against her cheek. "There could be a lot of explanations."

"Yeah, I know. But that one jibes with history. There was a lot of violence when the Cherokees were rounded up."

"Well, could be that soldiers came into the house after the family left," Drake offered. "And shot the place up just for the hell of it. One of them could've left a jacket behind. The jacket rotted but the buttons didn't."

"But I thought white settlers took over the deserted houses and cabins," Kat said. "Why would they let this one sit here until it fell down?"

Nathan stroked her cheek. "Justis owned it, remember? Nobody'd try to move into the house if the place was claimed by an important man like him."

"Great," Kat said bitterly. "So the only thing that saved the place was the fact that he stole it from great-great-grandmother's family. Real noble of him. I wonder why he didn't move his white wife up here. Hell, maybe he did."

"Aw, Katie, it wasn't like that."

Kat stared at him. Whenever he spoke in that strange, certain way, calling her Katie, a feeling of trust came over her.

His eyes locked on hers as if he were trying to remember something and looking at her helped. "Don't know," he said after a few seconds, wearily, and the intensity faded from his eyes. "It just seems to me that Justis was most likely a decent man. Maybe I want to like him for your sake."

She smiled a little then. "That's a good enough reason for me, sweetcakes."

"Let me take these buttons and musket balls into town," Drake told them. "There's a gun shop there run by an old codger who knows local history. He might confirm the button ID."

"Yeah, okay," Nathan answered. Looking at Kat, he said, "I'll walk to camp and bring back some lunch. Why don't you sit down and prop your ankle up on something?"

She nodded. "I'd kinda like to be alone here for a while." Kat looked around wistfully. "To think."

Drake got into at mud-spattered Jeep and drove away. Nathan hugged her tenderly, then swung off down the front side of the ridge, his proud, athletic stride holding her gaze until he was hidden by the trees.

Kat sat down on a log and stretched her injured leg out. Well, she had Nathan, she had her land, and even if there was a lot of sadness connected to her family's history she was going to love living here.

Especially if Nathan would live here with her.

Kat propped her chin on her hands and stared at the ground, trying to re-create the Blue Song house from its ghosts, wondering what had happened the day the soldiers came. How had Katlanicha escaped? When had she met Justis? Some things would always be a mystery.

A few minutes later she lifted her head at the

sound of a vehicle driving up the trail. Hmmm, Drake must have forgotten something.

But the car that pulled to a stop a few yards away from her sitting place was a fancy, late-model station wagon. And the person who got out was not Drake.

Kat rose in surprise as a statuesque, curvaceous young woman came toward her, head up, eyes imperious, majestic even in soft leather boots, jeans, and a ruffled white blouse. The woman's dark eyes and ethnic features, her bronzed skin and long black hair convinced Kat she was about to meet a fellow Indian—and an extraordinary-looking one.

"Hi ya," Kat said, cheerfully impressed by the stranger. This babe could make a mint if she ever wanted to wrestle.

The woman stopped less than two feet from Kat, tried to freeze her with a dignified glare, and said softly, "Tell me where he is, and then get out of my sight."

Seven

Shock made a raw and brassy taste in Kat's mouth. She jammed her hands into the front pockets of her cutoffs and the soft denim bunched under her clenched fingers.

"If you were important, I'd have heard about you," she told the woman.

Dark eyes gleamed fiercely. "Where is he?"

Kat shook her head. *Please, this isn't happening. Nathan couldn't have another lover.* She lifted her chin proudly. "I don't know what you were to him, but it's over now."

"Oh? Just let me talk to him. Is he even here, or did he desert you the way he deserted me?"

A tone of despair rang through the visitor's voice. Kat looked at her wretchedly. "He walked over to our, over there"—she pointed limply—"to get something from camp. He'll be back."

"Are you the one he bought the bra for?" The woman measured Kat's chest size with a gaze that held anguish. "No, you're too big." Her shoulders slumped and she said in a small, stunned voice, "Oh lord. He's got another one besides us."

Weak-kneed, Kat hobbled to the log and sank down numbly. "I don't believe it."

"Believe it. I saw the bra. It had a pink bow tied on it." Moving wearily, ramming her hands through hair even longer than Kat's, the woman lowered herself to the ground and sighed in defeat. "How long have *you* known him?"

"A few weeks." Kat tried to ignore the dread knotting her stomach. "How about you?"

"A few weeks. He left without saying good-bye— three weeks ago. I thought he'd come back, until I heard about you."

They traded stricken looks. The visitor shook her head and struggled noticeably not to cry. "I've known other white men who had a thing for Indian women, but I thought he was different. I thought he was sincere when he said he loved me."

Kat wanted to die. Nathan had never said that to *her*. "I just cannot buy this story," she said with renewed defensiveness.

"Me either," the woman said with a catch in her voice. "He seemed so special. I've never met anyone like him before. I mean, it was like I'd known him all my life."

Kat covered her face. "Oh no, it's true."

"I'm from the reservation up in North Carolina. Where are you from, around here?"

"Miami."

The woman made a soft sound of misery. "He *said* that he traveled a lot."

Kat got up and moved away, trembling. "I can't talk about this anymore. I don't want to be bawling my eyes out when he comes back."

"No." The visitor sniffed tearfully. "You're right."

"I guess we should introduce ourselves," Kat said, her throat on fire. "My name's Kat Gallatin."

"I know. Erica's cousin." She held her head and looked at Kat with despair. "I'm Echo Tall Wolf."

"Not from Grandpa Sam's family!"

"Yes."

"Oh no!" Kat hugged herself to keep from crying out loud and turned her back. "N-no more talk."

"R-right."

Kat limped farther from her and leaned rigidly against a dogwood tree. She and Echo Tall Wolf waited in silent, shared misery that seemed to last an eternity.

Finally Kat heard the rugged sound of a powerful engine and knew that Drake Lancaster was returning. She turned around and saw Nathan top the ridge, his knapsack hanging jauntily over one shoulder.

Great timing, harmonica man, she thought. Now Drake can be our audience.

She walked over to Echo, who got up hurriedly, brushing leaves from her jeans and looking from the approaching Jeep to Nathan. "I guess we're going to have an audience," she said grimly.

"Yeah. A friend of his."

"Well, it couldn't be any worse than it is already."

They stood side by side, waiting.

After he studied Echo Tall Wolf for a second, Nathan looked at Kat quizzically. His stride casual, he never faltered. Kat couldn't take her eyes off his lean, tanned body covered only by shorts and hiking boots, the body he'd shared with Echo Tall Wolf only a few weeks ago. She was dimly aware of the Jeep door slamming as Drake Lancaster got out.

"He's always so damned calm," Echo murmured hoarsely.

"Yeah." Kat gritted her teeth. Nathan didn't look more than a tiny bit intrigued to see two of his lovers waiting where only one had been before.

Drake strode toward them, frowning, one enormous hand clenched lightly over the front of the T-shirt he'd donned for the trip to town. He and Nathan reached them about the same time and stopped.

"Who'd you give the bra to?" Kat asked coldly. "You know, the bra with the pink bow on it?"

"Bra?" Nathan asked.

"What kind of work do you really do?" Echo interjected.

Kat touched her arm and their eyes met. "He's a geologist."

Echo gasped. "He told me that he was a biologist studying pollution for the forestry service."

"What are you talking about?" Nathan demanded.

Drake gestured for attention. "The bra was for Tess Gallatin."

Kat and Echo wailed at approximately the same time.

"Thanks for telling me the truth," Kat muttered. "Somebody needs to." She sighed heavily. "My cousin Tess. My own cousin. Poor Tess probably didn't know there were other women, either."

"I'm sure your cousin Erica would have told me if she'd known," Echo said. "But even Erica thought I should have faith."

Kat trembled. How did Drake know about the bra? Oh no! Holding out her hands in supplication, she asked Nathan, "Do you guys discuss *everything* about your women?"

"No, wait, I'm—" Nathan began.

"How could you say that you weren't involved with anyone but me," Echo demanded, "when all the time you and Tess Gallatin were meeting in some cave in the woods? How could you do that to me? How could you do that to Kat?"

"Hold on," Drake said. "I—"

"Please be quiet," Kat told him. The man had no business butting in. "Echo?"

She looked at Echo, who explained raggedly, "In the morning he'd say that he had work to do, then he'd ride a horse off into the mountains and come back late in the afternoon. He and Tess were sharing a cave, a *cave*."

Kat looked at Nathan tearfully. "Do you get your jollies livin' with Cherokee women in the woods?"

Nathan dropped his knapsack. Gazing at her openmouthed, he held up both hands in defense. "I am totally confused."

"Please tell me this isn't true."

"Tell us *both*," Echo added fiercely.

"Dammit," Drake said loudly, "I don't know what's going on here, but there's no other woman!"

"How do *you* know?" Kat demanded.

"I'd remember if there was more than one who could cause this much trouble!"

"I would, too," Nathan said blankly. "Especially if I knew what the hell we were talking about."

Kat pressed a fist to her lips. Sorrow nearly strangled her. "I wish you'd tell the plain truth. I only want to hear, 'Yes, right before I met you I was involved with Echo Tall Wolf,' or 'No, I wasn't.' "

Drake suddenly seemed a foot taller. "*What*?" he asked softly, with a lethal tightening of his body.

"Yes," Echo agreed with fierce control, "Just say it—did you leave me for Kat?"

Nathan's eyes turned the color of dark storm clouds. He gazed at Drake very, very intensely, as if waiting for answers. Drake returned the look in kind.

Kat was so upset that a stab of confusion was forgotten right after she noticed it. "Drake," she said as calmly as she could, "this is sort of private. Could you leave us alone with Nathan?"

"No, we're talking to Drake. You mean Drake," Echo interjected.

"No, I mean"—Kat turned to stare up at her—"I mean Nathan."

"Drake," Echo said softly, her dark eyes wide.

Kat shook her head slowly. Her heart was denting the inside of her chest. "Nathan."

Echo pointed a trembling finger. "You and Nathan?"

Kat nodded. "You and Drake?"

Echo nodded. "I came down here because Grandpa said Drake was in Gold Ridge with you."

"He works with Nathan. Nathan asked him to come here."

Echo clasped both hands to her heart and stared at Drake Lancaster, a desperate expression on her face. "*Colanneh,* I'm sorry I doubted you."

Kat made a strangled sound and didn't know whether she felt like laughing or hiding in embarrassment. Nathan's angry gaze told her laughter was *not* an option.

Echo continued to stare at Drake, who surveyed her with a troubled gaze. "What was I supposed to think after you disappeared without saying good-bye?" she asked softly.

"I left word that I'd be back. I said you had nothing to worry about. Why didn't you believe me?"

Echo shook her head. "Too many mysteries."

Drake stuck out a hand. "Come with me." To Nathan he said, "We'll be back after I explain a few things."

"Fine." Nathan's voice was flint-hard, and he spoke without taking his accusing gaze off Kat's repentant one.

"It wasn't Kat's fault," Echo called as Drake led her to the Jeep. "It was all so confusing."

Nathan didn't speak again until after Drake and Echo drove away. Then, his eyes full of reproach, he said, "I don't know how this mess started, but I do know that you don't trust me worth a damn."

"Aw, Nathan, I *do.* It was a misunderstanding—a strange woman comes here looking for the man who deserted her, and she never mentions a name, and how was I supposed to know that she'd known Drake up in North Carolina?"

"But the first thing you thought was 'Nathan lied to me.' "

Kat lifted her chin and eyed him proudly. "No, not

that. I've never asked you for any promises and you've never said I was the only woman in your life. I know better than to expect too much."

"Then why'd you make a fool out of yourself—like I belonged to you?"

Kat realized that she'd talked herself into a corner, and in doing so she'd provoked the truth from Nathan. He didn't want her to be possessive, or he wouldn't have asked his question so fiercely.

"For as long as you're part of this"—she gestured weakly at the land—"I feel like you belong to me."

He searched her face, his gaze shuttered. "Sounds like you only care about the land."

Words caught inside Kat's throat. "No, I care about you a lot, but I know the land will always be here, and you won't."

"You watch out for yourself first," he said between clenched teeth. "That's a smart way to live. That's the way I like to live, too."

Later, she would replay those words and die a thousand small deaths. But right now she had to salvage as much time with him as she could. "You're welcome to stay here as long as you want," Kat assured him. "I love . . . your company."

"Good. Real good," he said, breathing harshly, with something tormented and urgent rising in his eyes. "I'll be around here a lot—probably a hell of a lot more than you will be, for the next, oh, twenty years."

Kat shook her head, feeling dazed. "What are you talking about?"

He swept a hand at the magnificent woods, at the Blue Song homesite, at the valley and stream. "I own all the mining rights. I've waited a long time to dig the gold out of this land."

As she backed away, her hands pressed to her mouth, he added hoarsely, "And believe me, you won't want to live here then."

"You can't own the mining rights."

"Holt Gallatin signed them over to my great-grandfather in 1910." His voice was harsh, but sorrow clouded his eyes. "A ninety-nine-year lease. All mineral rights. The Gallatin family doesn't even get a percentage of the profits."

"No!"

He held out his hands to her. "Kat, I didn't mean to tell you like this. Dammit, I wanted to wait until you—"

"Were so crazy about you that I'd be on your side! Everything you've done—buying me things, acting like every word I said was important, doing all those things to please me in bed—it was only to get me on your side!"

"Dammit, no."

"Just like ol' Justis must have done to my great-great-grandmother! What a joke that must have been to you!"

Full of tension, he stepped forward swiftly and grabbed her arms. "I wanted you on my side, sure, because I didn't want to hurt you this way. I care about you too much to watch you lose everything you've dreamed about."

"But that won't stop you from taking it!"

He shook her lightly. His voice was agonized. "I promised my grandpa. I promised myself for my father's sake. It's something I've gotta do."

Shock and disappointment whirled in her head until she could barely think. "I trusted you. I trusted you in ways I've never trusted a man before."

"You still can."

She pulled away from him and pressed her hands to her temples. "I don't understand how you got our mineral rights. And what's your grandpa got to do with it? How'd my family hurt him?"

Nathan reached for her hand. "Let's sit down."

"I can't sit down." She stepped back. "Don't touch me."

He stood there looking as miserable as she felt. "You gonna listen? Listen good, so maybe you can understand that I'm not a greedy bastard looking for excuses to tear up this land."

"I'll give it a try," she shot back. "Talk."

"Holt Gallatin—Blue Fox—took up a one-man war against my family," Nathan told her. "After he killed my great-great-grandpa Nathaniel, the one who fought against Justis Gallatin in the Civil War, Holt went on the lam. Had to, since he was wanted for murder.

"The Indian Territory wasn't much more than a lot of empty land with plenty of places to hide, and there weren't enough U.S. marshals to track down a smart man who had help from the Keetowahs."

"The Cherokee society that hated white people?"

"Yeah. So Holt was able to ride over into Arkansas, strike at my family, and then go back to the Cherokee Nation and hide with hardly any chance of getting caught. He and a gang of Keetowahs robbed and murdered all over western Arkansas for almost twenty years. And the Chathams were their prime targets."

"You mean Holt killed other Chathams besides Nathaniel?"

"No, but he wounded a few and crippled one. And he tried to ruin any business a Chatham touched. He stole cattle, burned down stores, robbed a bank managed by a Chatham—in short, he was a curse that plagued my family for two decades."

"Then what?" she asked wearily, hugging herself.

"U.S. marshals chased him out of the Territory. Whites were moving in; there was talk about statehood—"

"The government was stealing land from the Indians again."

Nathan nodded slowly. "Yeah. I'm afraid that's right."

"So the thieves chased a thief off."

"A murderer," Nathan corrected, but without victory. "Holt was a bad man, one of the worst, Cherokee or white."

Kat slowly walked to an old tree and leaned against its gnarled trunk. Her eyes burning, she stared up into the thick foliage as if seeing something besides Nathan's grim face when he told her he intended to mine her land. "What happened after Holt left the Territory?"

"He disappeared for the next twenty years. I guess everyone in my family thought he was dead."

Nathan kicked at a broken limb on the ground. "But then Holt showed up again. He was getting old, he wanted to settle down on some land Justis and Katherine left him, and he had a young wife and two children—your grandpa Joshua, and Dove." Nathan looked disgusted. "Holt had wrangled some sort of amnesty from the U.S. government. I don't know how he did it, other than that his brother had some influence in Washington."

Kat nodded. "Silas Gallatin. He was Tess's great-grandfather. I think he became a pretty important man out in California."

"Holt didn't think his family would be safe in Oklahoma with a whole bunch of angry Chathams just across the Arkansas border. He wanted to bribe my family into forgiving and forgetting."

Kat groaned in frustration. "So he bargained with Eli Chatham or great-grandpa—for peace."

"Right. Holt gave him the mining rights to Katlanicha's land in Georgia. This land."

"But you said that Holt killed Eli."

Nathan laughed grimly. "He did, about ten years later. Those two old men never stopped hating each other. Holt came to Arkansas and called Eli out. They had a gunfight—one of the last bona fide, Main-Street-at-dawn-duels in the state of Arkansas. 1921. It made the local newspapers."

Nathan paused, and she looked at his brooding expression carefully. "And what happened to my great-grandpa then?"

"Nothing. He was shot, too. He died a few days after the fight."

Kat sagged inwardly and sat down on an exposed root at the base of the tree. "So your grandpa wanted revenge for his daddy, Eli's death. Why didn't he mine our land himself?"

Nathan came close and squatted down on his heels. Gazing into her eyes with a sorrowful expression on his face, he said softly, "Because Dove Gallatin was his mistress and he never stopped loving her."

"Oh no, no." Kat stared at him as a sick feeling of defeat grew in her stomach. "Not Dove. Erica told me all about her. She was an old maid. She lived in North Carolina."

Growing agitated, Kat waved her hands anxiously and rushed on without pausing for breath. "Everyone loved her. They said she had powers. When she got too old and sick to be happy, she willed herself to die. She left us each a family medallion because she *cared* about the Gallatin family—"

"Whoa, whoa. That may be all true—except she was no old maid." Nathan sighed, gazed at the ground, and ran a hand through his hair as he thought for a moment.

"Don't try to be nice," Kat said fiercely. "You and me got no reason to be nice to each other anymore. Just say it like it is."

He looked up at her with anguished, angry eyes. "Right. All I know is what Grandpa Micah told me, and he was no saint, at least not by the time I came along. Dove and him carried on for years behind my grandmother's back. Dove got pregnant, and out of spite she went to my grandmother and told her about the whole affair."

"I can't believe this," Kat whispered.

"Believe it. My grandmother killed herself over it. She left a baby son behind."

"Your father," Kat supplied weakly.

"Yep. My father. Grandpa Micah felt so guilty over what he'd done to his wife that he went straight to hell in a liquor bottle."

"What happened to Dove?"

"She ran off to England with an RAF pilot she knew from God knows where. Married him."

"And her baby?"

"Died of whooping cough before it was four. The pilot was killed during World War Two. That's all I know about Dove. She ruined my grandpa and deserted him."

Kat dug her nails into her palms. "So this Gallatin-Chatham feud came closer to you than I knew. It *is* personal."

He nodded, his cold gray eyes directly on hers. "My daddy had a drunk for a father. Grandpa lost just about everything he owned; he didn't give a damn how his son grew up, and because of that my daddy grew up worthless. He was a no-account drifter and he died in a bar fight when I was fifteen."

Even though this information about Nathan's background shocked her, she could only manage to retort, "Are you blaming my family for every rotten thing that ever happened to a Chatham?"

"I'm not blaming you or your cousins for anything. I'm simply saying that four generations of my family have been hurt by one Gallatin or another. It's only fair that this land should pay some of that debt back."

Kat stood up proudly. "We won't let you do this. You can't drag out a claim that our kin signed back when our grandparents were kids. It won't hold up in court."

He rose with slow, coiled emotion. "It's legal. I've had it checked out. There's not a damned thing you can do about it."

"I'm a fighter."

"You're a fake fighter. You put on war paint and play at being mean. This match against me is too much for you. Give it up."

He held out his hand to her suddenly, and Kat was surprised to see it tremble. "I'm not doing this for the money, Kat. I don't need the money. I do need you. I want us to be together despite this mining thing. I know that's a lot to ask."

"That's not just a lot to ask, that's impossible," she said softly, almost choking on the words. "My cousins would never forgive me and I'd never forgive myself. Oh, don't worry, I'm not through with you—not in court, anyway."

She left him standing there with his hand out as she walked away.

Depression created a filter around Kat, diffusing the world until nothing made much of an impression when it reached her eyes, her ears, her emotions.

"Erica?" Kat murmured into the phone, her voice raspy and low. She leaned wearily on the big antique desk that belonged to their lawyer in Gold Ridge, her shoulders slumped, her head down. Now she knew how warriors must have felt after a lost battle.

Drained, lifeless, empty.

"Kat? What's wrong? Are you sick? When I got your message I was worried. You sound sick."

Kat knew she wouldn't cry. She had only a few tears left, and she was too tired to use them. "There's something we never knew about the gold on our land. The lawyer didn't even know. I guess Dove Gallatin knew—maybe she thought we could fix the problem."

"Whatever it is, relax," Erica said patiently. "Our Cherokee relatives are buried on that land. Katherine Blue Song's family—her parents and three sisters. Tess's medallion says so. Grandpa Sam just finished deciphering it. I don't see how we can lease the mining rights, knowing that, so it doesn't matter about the gold."

Kat found her last tears. "Erica, we don't have any say-so over the mining rights. We never have."

"*What?*"

"My great-grandfather"—Kat paused to exhale heavily. "Holt Gallatin, he was trying to bribe his way out of trouble, so he signed the rights over to a man named Eli Chatham. A ninety-nine-year lease. There are twenty years left on it."

"Oh, Kat, no. I can't believe Dove's father would do that! Listen, Dove wrote down a lot of family history. It's all in Cherokee, and Grandpa Sam is still working on it. But I do know this much—Dove could predict the future. Dove wrote a poem about me that came true."

"Erica, I don't believe in all that kind of stuff."

"Dove gave us our medallions for a reason, Kat. Mine says that our great-great-grandmother went on the Trail of Tears to Oklahoma, with the rest of the tribe, but Justis rescued her."

"Oh, Erica, Justis didn't care about Katherine—Katlanicha."

"Yes, he did. I'm convinced of that. There's so much love in those medallions, Kat. Mine also says, 'A wolf will find his mate, no matter how far she roams.' Kat, I'm going to marry James Tall Wolf. Do you understand? My medallion held a prophecy."

Kat pounded a fist on the desk. "Erica, you're not listening."

"I don't know what Tess will make of hers. I've sent it back to her with the translation of the message. We'll just have to wait and see how she reacts. When Grandpa gets your medallion figured out, I think we'll see some kind of pattern. We were meant to have the land, we were meant to take care of it."

"My great-grandfather sold the mining rights and there's nothing we can do about it!" Kat yelled. "That's all that matters! He sold the rights to Eli Chatham. Later he and Chatham killed each other in a gun-fight. And now Chatham's grandson owns the rights!"

"Kat, honey, there has to be a way out of this," Erica said calmly, though there was a slight tremor in her voice. "Damn, I wish you weren't there alone. I can tell you're frantic."

"I'm sorry for yelling," Kat said hoarsely. "But listen, you don't understand. This isn't business, this is revenge." She explained the Gallatin-Chatham feud.

Erica groaned. "Kat, are you saying that this Chatham character blames us for all of that?"

"No, Nathan's real sorry for us, but he promised his grandpa, and he has a lot of honor."

"Whose side are you on?"

Kat felt a cold, shriveling pain wrap around her rib cage. "Ours. I'm a Gallatin. I gotta put the land first."

Erica asked gently, "Is there something I ought to know about you and Nathan Chatham?"

Swiping at her eyes, Kat exhaled sharply and said, "Nah. Listen. Micah Chatham put it in his will that nobody could mine our land until after Dove died. Now Dove's gone, and Nathan Chatham says he's going to, to—" Her voice cracked. "Do you know what 'heap leaching' is?"

"Oh Lord," Erica said raggedly, and Kat realized that her cousin was crying, too. "He'll turn our land into a gravel pit full of chemicals." She took a calming breath. "James and I'll drive down to Gold Ridge tomorrow morning. We can buy this Chatham bastard off or stop him in court. Kat, I know we can."

"Sure. I'm staying at the Kirkland Inn. See ya there."

She hung up the phone and sat thinking dully, *There's only one chance of changing Nathan's plan, and I'm the only Gallatin who can take it.*

• • •

He would never forget this day, no matter how hard he might try—Kat's face when he'd told her the truth about his pledge to his grandfather, her wilted little questions, and finally the way she'd just turned and limped to her car, without looking back.

All of it was branded into him, and the brand would be painfully raw for a long, long time.

Nathan capped the bottle of bourbon and tossed it aside. He couldn't remember the last time he'd gotten drunk, but it'd probably been for a celebration of some kind. Well, that's what tonight was—a celebration of family revenge, family honor, and the evolution of Nathan Chatham, idealistic geologist, into Nathan Chatham, heartless bastard.

Nathan rubbed his face wearily, slung another piece of wood at his campfire, not caring that his boozy aim made it miss the fire entirely, and stretched out on his side, propped up on one elbow.

His head swam. He shut his eyes and saw Kat's face. No, Katie's face. More often than not he thought of her that way. How could he win her after today? How he could make her understand that nobody would ever love her more than he did, despite the debt he had to settle for his family?

She was meant to love him back, but like before, it would take time for her to admit that, maybe even to herself.

Love him like before? Nathan cursed softly and rubbed his forehead again, as if he could force thoughts that made sense inside his brain.

Katie, give me a chance, gal. Katie.

"Nathan."

He opened his eyes groggily and saw her kneeling on the ground near his feet. Startled, he looked at her without speaking, slowly taking in the fact that she'd walked a half mile through the woods at night, alone, to come to him, that she wore the white dress he'd bought her, and that she'd crimped her hair somehow so that it cascaded around her in ebony waves.

She was so beautiful that he ached inside, so unreal in the firelight that he rubbed his eyes and checked to make certain she was still there, her hands calmly in her lap.

Maybe he was looking at a wishful thought.

But she rested a hand on his leg, and her touch seared him even through his buckskin breeches. "I love you," she said in a firm, somber voice, her eyes never leaving his.

Nathan blinked twice, shook his head, and almost said *I love you* back. But then he remembered the look of desperation on her face earlier that day.

He laughed hoarsely. "You love this land."

"I love you *and* the land. That's why I'm asking you for a deal."

"Love." Nathan said something so obscene that her hand trembled on him and she looked a little frightened. "Don't ever use that word to me," he warned. "It has nothing to do with what you want."

"Okay. If it bothers you so much, then you'll never hear it from me again."

"Good." He eyed her wearily, with dismay, finally asking, "So what's your deal?"

"Anything you want from me, for as long as you want it. I'll go wherever you tell me to go, do whatever you want me to do, work for you, sleep with you, wash your truck, clean your house—I guess you've got a house somewhere, don't you?" She smiled, but to Nathan it just made her look sadder. "How many men would turn down a nice slave?" she asked.

He stared at her in amazement. "This man would. I remember you saying, 'I don't want to go through the rest of my life being used.' "

"It's not the rest of my life. It's for as long as you want."

Nathan leaned on both elbows and let his head drape back. It made him dizzy. What he was thinking made the sensation even worse. *I wanted you then, I want you now, I want you forever.*

"And I'd give back the mining rights to your land," he said, tilting his head forward.

"I don't expect you to do that, Nathan. I guess I understand why you've gotta do what your family deserves." Her voice sounded old, defeated. "But maybe you could postpone the mining for a few years. You know—give me and my cousins some time to enjoy the land.

"Maybe Tess and Erica will have kids. If their kids could see this, you know, if the next generation of Gallatin kin could get even one look at where their people came from, where they're buried—"

"What d'you mean?"

"Katlanicha's parents and sisters are buried here," she explained, looking away from his intense gaze. "If you could give us a few years, maybe we can find their graves and move 'em. Tess's and Erica's children could see the old homeplace, and then you could do what you had to do."

"What about your children?" he asked grimly.

She shook her head and met his gaze again. "I don't think my prospects are too good. I don't get to know men too easy and I'm not marrying another 'safe' one so I can have children."

"You got to know me pretty easily," he reminded her. The hurt, angry look in her eyes made him wince. "I didn't mean it as an insult. Why am I different?"

"You just are." She frowned, looked down at her lap, fidgeted a little, and said finally, "We're great together. You said you want things to be right between us again. I know you're crazy about me in bed. And you like teaching me how to be a Cherokee."

"So we can go on like before if I give you a deal on

the land?" he asked, feeling anger rise inside him like a snake. "You can fake it, even if you hate my guts?"

"I know how to make you laugh, and I won't get in your way much. If you want to travel to any of the crazy places you like to visit, you know I can go along and not be a wimp. How many women got so much to offer and ask so little in return?"

"You can fake it?" he asked again, his voice rising.

She shook her head. Her eyes were ancient and despairing. "I don't hate you. I couldn't do this if I didn't want things to be right between us, too. Maybe I hate myself for still wanting you."

His fury stalled, and he studied her shrewdly, wondering if she were telling the truth. If she was . . . Nathan felt his breath grow shallow with hope. He crossed his feet nonchalantly and tossed out, "I never kept a mistress before."

She shivered a little, but she looked him straight in the eye and said stoically, "Let's call it what it is. I wouldn't be your mistress. I'd be your whore."

The slow, sick press of air out of his lungs mingled with an admiration for her strength that made him want to cry. There was a great stillness in the atmosphere around them, as if the night had stopped to listen.

"I don't see it that way. I see it as a friendly compromise between two people who need to be together."

"Then you're sugarcoating it to be nice. Don't get me wrong, there're plenty of ways to be a whore in this world, and they don't have anything to do with sex. I've seen people trade themselves for a lot of bad reasons. At least I'm doing it for a good one."

"I don't want you on those terms. I want you as a friend and lover."

"Okay, if that's how you look at it."

He struggled not to pound a fist against the earth and tell her that he wanted her to love him despite this nonsense between their families. *She's giving you a chance to win her over. Don't be a fool. Take it.*

"What if I tell you to do things that you've never done before?" he asked, giving her a hard, slit-eyed appraisal. "Things that might embarrass you, things that would please me a whole hell of a lot more than they would you. You gonna do 'em?"

"Yeah." She rubbed her hands up and down her palms, and he saw goose bumps on the honey-colored skin.

"You might learn to like 'em."

"Sure. You won't get any trouble from me."

"All right. I'll take your deal. You're mine, body and soul, for as long as I want. Starting tonight. Tomorrow I'll have a lawyer draw up a contract."

"I trust your word."

"You're awful magnanimous."

"I don't know what that means, but I guess it's good." She was trembling noticeably now. "I only have one condition. I don't want my cousins to know I've got this deal with you. They'd try to stop me. I'll just tell 'em that I talked you out of mining our land right away."

Nathan chuckled harshly. "So you three Cherokee musketeers will have years to attack my mining rights with every legal maneuver you can find."

She looked at him for a moment, then said softly, "Yeah, that's the way I'm figuring it."

"All right. I like your honesty. You belong to me. Our secret. In return you get a five-year grace period for your land. Deal."

"Deal."

He slipped the gold nugget from around his neck and handed it to her. "I want you to wear this all the time."

Her eyes gleamed with surprise. She took the sturdy gold chain and pecan-sized nugget, cupped them in her hand for a moment, then slipped the chain over her head.

Nathan caught his breath. The gold seemed to gleam brighter just from being close to her. He squinted, shook his head to clear it, but couldn't rid himself of the illusion.

It was only right that she have the nugget, right that the warmth of her spirit should make it take on new life. After all, it was the one thing he could give back. It had belonged to Justis Gallatin.

Eight

The frigid mountain water cut through her brooding thoughts and made her think only of getting warm again. That, unfortunately, made her think of Nathan's leg draped across her thighs and his arm lying relaxed and possessive under her breasts.

Kat put her soap and shampoo on a rock, sat down close by, and curled her legs to one side. Water closed around her waist, the stream capturing her, making her a part of the land it served.

She scooped water onto her face and held it there, the silver drops draining down her arms like tears. This bargain would ruin her, because unless Nathan fell in love with her somewhere along the way, she'd lose both him and any chance of saving the land.

The thought of losing either made her whimper softly; more so because it was Nathan she needed most.

"Kat."

She jerked her head up and looked over her shoulder. He waded across the stream to her, naked, carrying a towel in one hand with little regard for whether it hid anything or not.

He dropped the towel next to her shampoo and sat down behind her in the stream. His hands cupped her shoulders. "Morning."

"Morning."

"Why are you crying?" he pulled her hair back and cupped her chin in one hand, holding her face in profile as he studied it.

"I just splashed water on my face."

"I don't want you to go around miserable."

"Okay."

He rested a hand along her cheek, his fingertips trailing over her skin as she faced forward again. "I don't want you to ask me for permission to get out of bed, either."

"Okay, I won't do it again."

"I want things to be like they were between us before. Like there was no bargain. 'Cause there isn't a bargain. There's only a compromise between . . ."

"Two people who need to be together. I know. Okay."

His fingers curved over her shoulders and shook lightly. "Stop that. Stop agreeing to everything like you don't have a choice."

"What kind of choice do I have? I already said I'd do whatever you tell me, and you already said I wouldn't like some of it."

"I didn't do anything you hated last night, did I?" He pushed her hair aside and slid his hands down her back, stroking her spine with his thumbs.

"You were full of bourbon. You fell asleep five seconds after you grabbed me."

"Grabbed you?" he repeated drolly.

"Yeah. I felt like a teddy bear."

"Whatd'you think I was going to do?"

"Something besides fall asleep."

"Disappointed?" He soaped his hands and began washing her back, sliding his fingertips in slow circles.

"I don't know. Everything's so different between us now."

He stopped washing and rested his forehead against the back of her head. His hands closed around her arms. "Tell you what, Kat Woman. I'll treat you like a teddy bear until you're ready to stop thinking that way. You say when."

Breathing quickly, a familiar tickle of desire growing in her stomach, Kat knew that she'd be ready soon. His concern for her happiness pretty much destroyed any doubts she'd had about his motives. Yes, Nathan cared about her, and he was willing to do anything to make her forget about the land problem.

She'd never forget, though. It would always be between them. But she hadn't been lying to him last night when she'd said that she wanted things to be right again, too. She didn't think they ever would be, but she had to try.

Her throat closed with anger. He could afford to be that word, *magnanimous*. He held everything in the palm of his hand—the future of the land, her future, her love.

"What if I'm never ready to make love to you again?" she asked.

He laughed softly and reached for the shampoo. "You will be 'fore too long," he promised, as his hands sank into her hair.

Kat and Erica sat in the Kirkland's intimate country tearoom at the same window table where they'd first discussed Dove's legacy, two months earlier, except that Tess wasn't with them. Beyond the window with its curtains of white eyelet the dogwood tree that had reached out to them with delicate blossoms now stroked its lush summer foliage against the panes, as if seeking to come indoors from the August heat.

Erica, tall and lanky, had changed over two months in subtle ways that Kat took a moment to analyze; it wasn't simply that she'd switched her unflattering gray suit for a tailored white dress or that she now used combs to pull her chestnut hair back from her face; it was her aura of happiness.

The source was no mystery. Ten minutes ago James Tall Wolf had left the tearoom to call his attorney about the mining agreement Holt Gallatin had signed with Eli Chatham. James was certainly tall and certainly one heck of a handsome, well-dressed wolf.

Kat had watched Erica's loving gaze track him all the way from the room. He'd stopped in the doorway to offer her one last bit of reassurance in the form of a wink and a smile.

Now *this* was how two people acted when they loved each other.

Kat reminded herself that Nathan's gold nugget was hidden under her T-shirt. It meant a lot, his giving her that piece of gold to wear. Of course, it was sort of like a collar on a slave, but she wouldn't think about that too much.

"I wish Tess were here, too," Erica noted, looking out the window at nothing. "But I don't think she's back in the country yet."

Kat shook her head in awe. "Should we call her Princess Tess now, ya think?"

Erica sighed. "I don't know. Until this problem came up with Nathan Chatham, I couldn't wait to see her and find out how she learned that her mother was queen of Kara. Now I can only think about our land."

Erica cleared her throat, reached into a large white purse, and retrieved a page torn from a magazine. "I have some information on Nathan Chatham for you."

Her voice was somber, almost regretful as she handed Kat the page. "I found it in an old issue of *Forbes.*"

Hands trembling, Kat laid the glossy, important-looking page on the table and stared incredulously at a color photograph of Nathan lounging in a cushy executive office, his moccasined feet propped up on a gleaming desk. Behind him a wall-sized window framed the unmistakable skyline of downtown Atlanta —the tall cylinder of the Peachtree Plaza Hotel, the Hyatt Regency with its famous restaurant room on top looking like a flying saucer that had landed on the hotel's roof.

Nathan wore tan trousers and a blue cashmere pullover similar to the one he'd had on the night she'd landed in his lap at the wrestling arena. His slight smile was confident; his spaniel eyes were half-shut in a knowing look; he was the essence of relaxed power. The cutline underneath confirmed it.

Chatham's New Age sensibilities and old-fashioned business sense win him raves from environmentalists and a fortune from gold mines.

"A fortune?" Kat repeated, frowning. "He might own our mining rights, but he's still just a geologist for Tri-State."

"No," Erica said softly. "He owns Tri-State. In fact, he owns the company that owns Tri-State."

After staring at Erica for several seconds while her mind tried to comprehend, Kat numbly looked down at the page and read, "This boy wonder has changed the nature of gold mining and reaped $300 million for Auraria, Inc., a company he started twelve years ago when Suradoran Indians led him to a vein of gold in the Amazon river basin.

"In a cooperative effort that has become his trademark, Chatham made money for both himself and the tribe, which has used its newfound wealth to bring the best of modern living to its people, while preserving ancient traditions. Twenty years from now, when the Suradoran site is mined out, Auraria, Inc., will restore the site fully. Unlike smelter refining, Auraria's heap-leaching method leaves virtually no permanent toxic effects."

"He sounds like an admirable man," Erica allowed. "Except in our situation."

Kat read the words again, then once more, then out loud. Then she stared blankly out the window and thought, *No wonder he has a nice truck.* That was the only way she could define $300 million.

"Ladies!" a voice called in a lilting English accent. "I understand from our charming lawyer that you can't wait to tell me something! I have quite a story, too!"

Kat and Erica twisted in their chairs to gaze at the elegant, darkly exotic young woman who smiled at them affectionately as she floated into the room close beside a ruggedly beautiful blond man.

Her eyes shining with joy, Tess Gallatin introduced her cousins to Jeopard Surprise, whom she described as "the man I adore entirely too much for his ego's good," a comment that made his rather guarded expression soften with pleasure. Kat noticed that he watched Tess with loving pride as she returned hugs and excited greetings.

Tess chuckled. "I've told him all about our land and our marvelous heritage. And I can't wait to tell you two about the winery Justis and Katherine started in California during the 1840's. It's all so romantic and exciting."

Kat and Erica traded sympathetic looks. Kat patted Tess's arm wistfully. "We better order a whole pot of tea, English. You're gonna need it."

Shirtless, dressed in his buckskin breeches and hiking boots, the tiny gold nugget gleaming in the top of his ear, sweat and grime streaking his hairy chest, Nathan was not what people expected a multimillionaire gold-mining executive to look like. Kat's heart rate accelerated at the memory of his slow, thorough attention to her hair that morning. Only

Nathan could make her feel that she'd been satisfied as well as shampooed.

Kat was surprised to find him and Drake at work again on the Blue Song homeplace, with Echo clucking around behind them, picking up the things they unearthed, a large brown hen instead of a small one, Kat noted wryly.

"That's Chatham?" Tess said in amazement, as Kat guided the Mustang to the end of the old trail. Tess sat in the front passenger seat, or more precisely, in Jeopard's lap. Erica had her legs across James's lap in the Mustang's small backseat.

It was a good thing everybody was in love, Kat thought.

"Yep. He's, uhmm, he's sorta different. He's not such a bad guy. Like I told you, he helped me find the old Blue Song place."

"Drake!" Tess exclaimed, as the black-haired giant stepped forward and scrutinized their arrival. She turned her head and looked at Jeopard closely.

"This is news to me," he responded.

"Drake does some security work for Nathan Chatham's company," Erica commented from the backseat. Her voice was puzzled. "You know him, Jeopard?"

Kat glanced at Jeopard Surprise. "You know Drake?"

He smiled, revealing practically nothing, while Tess fiddled with the collar of his white polo shirt and was much less successful at looking inscrutable.

"Drake works for Jeopard sometimes, too," Tess said pleasantly. "They're old friends in the security business."

James, who'd been ominously silent since noticing Drake Lancaster, asked in a soft, grim tone, "Can my sister trust him?"

Jeopard didn't hesitate. "Drake would die for her. Yes, she can trust him."

"He has very good taste in women's lingerie," Tess quipped.

As everyone got out of the car Nathan tossed his

shovel down, slipped a T-shirt over his torso, and strode over to greet them. He met Kat's eyes, and his somber gaze seemed to say, "So the war party's finally here."

Kat introduced him and watched her cousins' expressions carefully. They didn't think of Nathan as a monster, since she'd told them about his Cherokee knowledge and sympathies, but they didn't want him to destroy their land any more than she did.

Drake and Echo walked up. Looking contented, Echo strolled to her brother, and gave him a hug.

"Happy?" he asked.

She said something in Cherokee, smiled, and went back to Drake's side.

"Kat says you're giving us a five-year grace period," Tess told Nathan. "Why?"

Kat clamped her hands together and wondered how Nathan would explain. She didn't want her cousins to think she was in cahoots with him, maybe trying to get a share of the Blue Song gold. They must never find out about her bargain.

"I have a lot of interest in your heritage," he explained calmly, nodding to Kat as if she could confirm that.

"So the Gallatins and the Chathams have always feuded?" Erica asked.

"Yep. From Justis and Nathaniel during the Civil War to Holt and Eli to Dove and Micah." Nathan shrugged and looked at Kat too innocently. "Who knows? We might be the ones to end the feud."

"Why are you doing all this excavation work?" James asked in a quiet, authoritative voice. "What do you expect in return?"

"Nothing. I like Kat. We're friends. I don't have anything against any of you folks. But mining this land is something I have to do for my family, just as you've got to take care of your family's interests. I've got a mining lease that's legal. The transaction was even recorded in the courthouse records up in Arkansas. You can't fight it."

"Oh, we can," Jeopard interjected pleasantly. He held out a hand to Nathan. "But thanks for helping my brother last year."

Kat pressed her fingers to her temples and watched as Nathan shook Jeopard's hand. What was this—a soap opera? Their lives had crossed one another's in such unusual ways before they'd all reached this common ground. Had Katlanicha expected this? Is that what the medallions were about?

"What does your medallion say?" she asked suddenly, turning toward Tess. "And did it mean anything to you?"

Tess smiled, and Kat noticed how Jeopard's hand strayed subtly into hers. "It said, 'A bluebird should follow the sun.' It brought me home to Jeopard."

Kat swallowed the lump in her throat. Tess's medallion had brought her to Jeopard; Erica's had brought her to James. "I bet when Grandpa Sam figures mine out it'll say something dumb like 'Buy two, get one free.' "

The smiles around her, including Nathan's, only made her feel worse.

With a few more Cherokees, they could start a village.

Everyone changed into casual clothes and came back to work on the excavation. It made Kat's chest swell with pride, watching her cousins and their men enjoy the discoveries as much as she had.

But it made her uncomfortable, too, having them so close to her and Nathan, having Nathan's necklace hidden under her shirt, trying not to look at him or touch him in any way that would reveal their true relationship.

Echo and Drake wouldn't talk; they'd already pledged their silence, though they didn't know about the bargain. What happened between a man and a woman was nobody's concern but their own, Echo had said solemnly. She and Drake, whom Echo now called *Colanneh*, the Raven, had agreed.

Nonetheless, Kat found that being around Nathan that day was difficult. The air always seemed a degree or two warmer between him and her, the emotions shimmering like an invisible web.

Heat. Lord, August was so sticky. Fanning herself, Kat left the homesite and walked past Nathan's truck to an ice chest Jeopard had brought in Gold Ridge. She got a soft drink, started to open it, then noticed a curious rock sticking up from the leaves a dozen yards away.

It had a rough square shape that made her wonder if it had been chiseled. Her drink in one hand, Kat traipsed over, still limping but not badly.

She reached the odd rock and saw that there was a large circle of similar rocks under the leaves. "Hey, guys!" she called, and putting her fingers to her lips, pierced the air with a whistle. "Look what I found!"

Then she stepped into the center of the circle, and the whole world gave way.

Cool. Damp. Close. Like a wet grave. Those reactions ran through Kat's mind as soon as she stopped falling. She looked up and found the top of the hole only a dozen feet overhead, but it might have been a mile.

Shaking, Kat laughed when she saw that she still held the soft drink can. She dropped it and hugged herself. This was no ordinary hole; it had carefully constructed rock walls. Under her feet—oh no, her injured ankle hurt like hell—the walls had caved in long ago, making a jumble of rock and mud.

Boots crashed through the leaves aboveground, followed by a louder crash as Nathan threw himself on his stomach at the edge of the hole. "Katie!"

"I'm okay."

"Get against the wall. I'm jumping down."

She pressed herself to flat stones and felt water trickle along her neck. Nathan rolled over the lip of the hole and dropped lithely beside her. They were chest to chest in the small area.

"Kitty Kat, I thought you'd lost one of your nine lives," he said gruffly, his hands stroking her head, cupping her face, then running down her arms as he tried to examine her in their narrow confines.

"I just hurt my ankle some." She wound her arms around his neck and he drew her close. Kat rested her head on his shoulder and wanted to cry, her emotions jarred free by the fall. "I need you," she whispered raggedly.

He brushed his lips over her hair and curved one hand over her head protectively. "I need you, too, gal."

"*Nathan*," a voice called in soft warning.

They looked up to find Drake peering at them anxiously. The others were coming. Quickly Kat stepped back as best she could. Nathan's fingers slid down her arm and he squeezed her hand in a silent good-bye.

Soon everyone was clustered around the hole. Nathan called up, "I'll put her on my shoulders and y'all lift her out."

"I'll do it," Drake said, and dangled a long arm the size of a tree toward them.

Kat laid her hands on Nathan's shoulders tentatively, as if she hadn't grown accustomed to caressing the ruddy skin under his T-shirt, as if her fingernails hadn't left marks in that skin at times.

"Can you climb onto my shoulders with your bad foot?" he asked.

"Us Flying Campanellis never forget how."

She scrambled up his body as if he were a ladder, almost smiling when her foot wedged a little too close to his groin. He muttered under his breath, "Wanta be a teddy bear the rest of your life?"

No, she thought with a fervor that shook her. She

wanted to be in his arms, away from everyone else, being doctored in his Cherokee ways and soothed in his other ways, ways that men in every culture knew—or ought to know.

Drake pulled her upward as if she were a feather. James grabbed her around the waist with hands that had once crushed quarterbacks in professional football, but held her delicately. Jeopard caught her legs and deftly swung them out, his easy grace making her feel as if she were Ginger and he were Fred in a strange sort of dance.

The men put her fanny-first on the ground and she sat there looking up expectantly as Erica and Tess hovered over her. "I haven't had so much fun since I tag-teamed with the Russian Roulette Brothers."

They laughed with relief.

"There's something down here!" Nathan called.

Kat was nearly the first one back at the opening. "You okay, sweetcakes?" she called, facedown at the edge of the darkness.

"Yeah."

"Sweetcakes?" Tess repeated.

"Sweetcakes," Erica mused.

"Aw, I call everybody that."

Nathan was on his knees, scooping mud from around the jumbled rocks. "It's a half-dry spring. Must of been a couple of feet deeper before it caved in. I think there's something wedged here, if I can just get it, there. Huh! A couple of spoons."

The sweetcakes business was temporarily forgotten as everyone crowded closer to the edge. "What are spoons doing in the bottom of a well?" Erica asked.

"Unless the Blue Songs dumped them there for a reason," James suggested. "Cherokee families hid what they could before the army came. If they were in a hurry they would have dumped things down the well."

"Get me a shovel!" Nathan called. "And a bucket!"

Tess and Erica nearly collided as they ran to get one. Kat started to rise, favoring her ankle. Nathan glanced up at her, said something jovial in Chero-kee, and Echo put a restraining hand on her shoulder.

"He says, 'Make the h·mmingbird keep her bent wing still.' "

Kat eyed him, then chuckled with helpless devo-tion. "Okay, you bossy gopher."

From the corner of her eye she saw Jeopard study-ing her expression. Kat looked up at him, and he smiled quickly, as if to put her at ease.

A thread of alarm trickled down Kat's spine. What would her cousins think if they realized that she loved the man who was going to tear up their land and steal their gold? She didn't want them to hate her or think she wanted the gold.

"Hey, Chatham," she called to Nathan in an ugly voice. "Don't slip any of our spoons into your pockets."

He stopped examining the blackened, corroded sil-verware and stared up at her as if she'd just threat-ened to bury him in the well.

"Are you serious?"

"You better believe it. The silverware's not yours just because it came out of the ground."

The slow tightening of his face and body assured Kat that she'd accomplished what she'd intended—she'd made him forget about being nice to her.

"I don't want anything but what's due my family," he said in a soft, lethal voice.

"I can't tell. You got mighty funny definitions of what's due your family."

He tossed the spoons up to her. "Take 'em. And leave me alone."

"Can do." Her throat tight with sorrow for them both, she left him in the old well glaring up at her.

The men took turns digging, and by late afternoon the women had scrubbed over forty pieces of silverware,

some bearing on their handles the still-legible Cherokee symbols for Blue Song. The heavy sterling was
ruined beyond anything except sentimental value, but
the cousins cried over the lost dreams it represented.

Then Jeopard's shovel found other pieces of sterling
—a tea set, a soup tureen, a tray so corroded that it
broke in two when he handed it out of the well.

"I hope there's no more," Kat said, her throat raw
as she watched Tess and Erica hug separate halves
of the tray. "This is like a funeral."

"Well, better find it all while you have the chance,"
Nathan warned. He stood on the sidelines, watching, his eyes cold.

"We've got five years," she shot back.

"Yeah. Consider yourself lucky."

He gave her a commanding look that reminded
her why they had five years, and she crumpled inside. Oh, he wanted her to think that he and she
had a friendly agreement, that he cared about her so
much that he'd postponed the mining.

But she wasn't supposed to forget that he could
change his mind if she didn't do exactly as she'd
promised.

I'm a slave, she thought again, and the gold nugget lying between her breasts made her chest move
heavily, as if it could smother her.

She awoke the instant she heard the soft rattle of
the key in the inn's old-fashioned door lock. Kat
scooted up in bed, reached frantically for the nightstand, then remembered that she'd left the Beretta
back in her tent.

But when the door opened, the faint light of a hall
lamp fell across Nathan's face—angular and harsh
in the shadows. Kat groaned softly with relief, her
heart still in overdrive.

"What are you doing here? My cousins have rooms
on either side of this one."

He shut the door, throwing the room into the deep ink of a moonless night. Kat quivered when she heard him lock the door. Then there was nothing but silence, a silence she listened to while breath pooled in her lungs.

Slowly he settled on the bed beside her, and she smelled the mingled traces of woodsmoke and a brisk, fresh scent that told her he'd scrubbed himself in the stream after everyone left.

"We can't sleep together tonight," she murmured, almost begging. "If my cousins figure us out they won't understand."

"Who said anything about sleep?" His voice was soft and gruff, whether from leftover anger she couldn't tell. "Lie back down."

Kat shut her eyes, analyzed the emotions that were making her vibrate with awareness, and admitted that she wanted him in bed with her, no matter what.

She slid down and put her hands beside her head on the pillow. His fingertips grazed her shoulder, skimmed over the soft cotton of her T-shirt, then trailed down her arm.

Kat tilted her head back on the pillow and heard herself breathing faster in the stillness of the room. It was an incredible sensation, to lie there in total darkness, knowing that Nathan was beside her but feeling only the provocative caress of his callused fingertips, not knowing what part of her he might touch next, or in what way.

He covered her hand with his, simply letting his hand rest there quietly atop hers, and the sensation was so exquisite that Kat made a soft keening sound.

"I don't mean to scare you," he said grimly.

"That wasn't fear you heard," she whispered. "I'm sorry I hurt your feelings today. I did it to make things easier in front of everyone."

"That's what I came here tonight to find out."

His hand tightened, then slowly slid away. A second later she felt its pressure on her stomach, his blunt, scarred fingers incredibly adept as they eased her panties down to her thighs, hardly brushing her skin, setting off storms of sensation when they did.

Kat bit her lip to keep from shifting in blissful agony as his hand touched her stomach again. This time there was the seductive whisper of cotton on her skin as he lifted her T-shirt, then the breath of night air scattering goose bumps on her bare stomach and breasts.

For a moment he stopped touching her at all, and it took considerable willpower for her not to reach for him. Then his fingertips surrounded her nipples with wetness from his mouth.

The combination was fire and ice as he rubbed them—just the tips, very slowly and very lightly—into peaks so hard they barely flexed under his caress.

"This woman is of the blue clan," he whispered. "Her name is Katlanicha. I am adopted of the deer clan, my name is Tahchee. Draw near to listen. Our souls have come together. I am *da-nitaka*, standing in her soul. She can never look away."

His fingers left her and she inhaled weakly, the sound a plea. A moment later, wet again, they slid between her thighs. He stroked the sleek skin and whispered over her soft cries, "Your body, I take it. Your flesh, I take it. Your heart, I take it."

He said those words again and again, a soft, guttural chant in rhythm with the movement of his fingers until sensation and sound mingled with the roaring in her ears and she heard nothing, knew nothing except waves of pleasure that made her body strain to follow the crests.

In the slow collapsing afterward, she heard him say, his voice tormented with restraint, "I am *da-nitaka*, standing in her soul. I have always been there. I will always be there. It was decided long ago."

Kat was still fighting for breath, her head lolled to

one side on the pillow, feeling the dampness of her perspiration, when he rose off the bed. She turned her face to search for him hopelessly in the darkness, then sensed him and lay still, poised for whatever he did next, whatever he asked, anything.

His mouth brushed hers, his mustache tickling her upper lip as he drew away. Kat waited, too limp to move, every ounce of her energy tuned to him. When he unlocked the door, slipped out, and locked it behind him, she exhaled so long and slow that her body seemed to melt into the bed.

Spellbound, she fell asleep just as he had left her.

When morning came she found a note from him on the bedside table. It told her what she had to do that day, and she wondered sadly if this was only the beginning of the requests she would not like.

Nine

Nathan certainly liked to stay on top of his job. In fact he lived on top of it in a penthouse complex with a Jacuzzi, a sun deck, rooms full of native artwork from all over the world, a master bedroom that rivaled something from a Moroccan fantasy, and a huge garden room that looked toward the cityscape of Atlanta.

No, it wasn't a garden room, Kat corrected herself as she stood in the midst of vine-draped tropical trees, it was a *jungle* room.

"Do you have everything you need?" Nathan's administrative assistant inquired politely, in a lyrical accent the Jamaican tourist bureau ought to hire.

Kat turned toward the young man, studied his jeans, sports shirt, and dreadlocks, then concluded that *maybe* she wouldn't feel out of place in Nathan's mixed-up business/fantasy world.

"Yeah, I'm fine. Thanks for carrying my duffel bag up."

"No problem." He handed her an envelope. "Key to the private elevator, key to the apartment door, a note with my phone extension downstairs. You're welcome to a tour of the company anytime. Just come on down."

"Thanks." No way, Kat added silently. The last thing she wanted was to be the prime source of gossip on five floors of Auraria, Inc.

After the assistant left she wandered around the huge apartment, listening to the lonely squeak of her Reeboks on polished slate, parquet, and hand-made Spanish tiles, her hands sunk in her jeans pockets because she was afraid to touch anything.

Not that Nathan's place looked formal—no, it was warm, exotic, inviting—but it was so damned *expensive*. His note hadn't warned her. It merely had told her to go to Atlanta, move into the apartment, and make herself at home.

Well, sure, but she'd never lived in a Native Peoples exhibit before.

Kat went into his bedroom and stared at rich wall hangings, rugs so deep she could get lost in them, and a big bed filled with fringed pillows and canopied in dark silks. If she tried to describe this room to anyone it'd either sound silly or self-indulgent, but it wasn't. It was incredibly masculine in a way that made her think of incense mingling with the erotic scent of seduction, of low-burning lamplight glistening on naked skin.

She sat down on the bed and burst into tears. It was a perfect place for a slave girl to please her master.

Where the hell was Nathan? she thought with unslavelike rudeness, wiping her eyes. He hadn't even said when he planned to follow her here, or even if he would follow. She still ached inside from telling her cousins a lie. They thought she was back on the wrestling tour, doing ringside commentary until her ankle healed completely.

Fifteen minutes later the phone rang. Kat sidled up to a heavily carved bedside table and gazed warily

at the black phone sitting there. It looked ordinary.
Well, at least she could touch this safely.

"Hi."

"Ms. Gallatin, I'm Cassandra, from Neiman-Marcus."

"Okay."

"Are you ready to go? I have a limousine waiting."

"Go where?"

"Shopping."

"I don't shop."

"Uhmm, Mr. Chatham says"—Kat heard the Cassandra person rattling a piece of paper—"he says
you're to spend at least three thousand dollars before the store closes this evening."

Kat sat down weakly and hugged a fringed pillow.
"Oh. How many hours have we got?"

"Five."

*That was six hundred bucks an hour. She'd
have to stand in the middle of the store and give
away cash.*

"I can't," she whispered.

"Mr. Chatham said you wouldn't have any problem with the plan."

"Oh." This was an order from Nathan, then. A
really odd kind of order. Was this another example
of the stuff she was supposed to do whether she
liked it or not?

Kat sighed. "I'll be right down."

As soon as I get over being shocked.

This was Nathan's guilt at work. He had a lot of
regrets where she was concerned, because of the
Blue Song land, and maybe his kindness was moti-
vated more by those than by affection for her.

Well, they'd play this game then, this sad game,
until one of them lost.

Nathan paused at the apartment's double doors,
his hand on the gold-plated doorknob, trembling. All
right, so he was bullying her. Yesterday's Neiman-

Marcus thing must have set her teeth on edge; he could only imagine what she'd thought when she got up this morning and found a man waiting downstairs to take her shopping for a new car.

But she'd get used to all that, she'd see what kind of life he could give her, and she wouldn't be able to resist. He'd dazzle her until she couldn't think straight, and then he'd marry her.

He'd donate all the money from the Blue Song mining operation to charity, so she and her cousins might eventually forgive him for turning their land into a huge gravel pit. Then her family would be happy, his family would be revenged, and Kat would love him as much as he loved her.

It was simple, Nathan thought. So why was he worried?

"Kat?" he called nonchalantly, as he strolled into the apartment. The lights were low, and through an arched doorway he could see that she'd shut the garden room blinds against the afternoon sun. He walked into a den done in Cherokee art, plush earth tones, and with a floor-to-ceiling stereo system.

The harmonies of a soft instrumental tape resonated through the room.

"Kat?" he called, and wondered grimly if concern made his voice sound little like Buckwheat's on *Our Gang.*

"Hi." She floated into the den from the hall that led to his bedroom. Her lithe little body was draped in nothing but a robe of pale green silk which matched her eyes; her hair had been curled and fluffed and moussed into one of those sexy "I've just come from bed" styles.

The gold nugget gleamed at the V of her robe, and small gold-and-jade studs decorated her earlobes. When she swept up to him and latched her arms around his neck, he inhaled a sensuous designer perfume, something with a decadent name, he figured.

"I'm glad you're finally here," she whispered, smiling.

Nathan didn't know if he liked what money had done to her basic feminine appeal, but he liked having her smile at him, and the knowledge that she was happy made him even more determined to keep her that way.

"Do you like—" he began, but she raised herself up and kissed him.

"I'm taking you to bed for the rest of the day," she whispered, and slipping her hand into his, she did just that.

Night was in the room when he woke, his body still heavy and satiated from everything she'd done so slowly and so well. Nathan sat up in bed, feeling silk sheets slide down his stomach the way Kat's hands had done earlier.

But Kat was gone.

He threw a dark russet kimono—a gift from a Japanese business associate—around his shoulders and left the room quickly, his heart pounding with a strange dread.

She's left me before.

Nathan exhaled raggedly when he found her curled, asleep, on an overstuffed couch in the den. She's left me before? Kat had never left him—and he'd make sure she never would. Shaking his head at the idea, he went to her and knelt down.

She wore one of her silly *WOW—Wild Women of Wrestling* T-shirts, with her green silk robe jumbled over her legs like a blanket. Her face was streaked with dried tears and her arms were wrapped around one of the rusty, pitted window sash weights from the Blue Song home.

Sorrow and confusion tore at Nathan. Then he realized what she'd done—she'd put on a grand show for him today because she thought she had to repay him for all the damned gifts.

He almost choked on the knowledge that she'd

made love to him for that reason. Oh, she hadn't faked her body's reaction, he was sure of that, but she'd faked her happiness.

His chest tightened with disappointment. Wearily he slid his arms under her. She stirred, then blinked up at him with swollen, worried eyes.

"Sssh," he said, because it was all he could manage easily.

Nathan carried her and her whimsical keepsake to bed. She held it, and he held her.

She woke with his lips brushing over her forehead gently. Kat blinked in the cozy light from a brass lamp beside the bed, then looked up into Nathan's eyes.

"Mornin'," he said softly.

"You found me out," she whispered. "I didn't mean to go to sleep on the couch."

But she had meant to cry. Her attempt at keeping her emotions in check had fallen apart yesterday.

She wanted to make him so happy that he'd fall in love with her and drop his mining plans completely. For that kind of result Kat figured she needed to stay cool, to play the seductress.

But the "cool" part of that plan had failed miserably. She'd heard herself calling his name and begging him for more. He'd turned her into a willing partner, and afterward she'd felt like a traitor for enjoying it.

"You can go to sleep anywhere you want," he assured her. "Long as I can find you."

Obviously he wasn't going to question her about the tears. He got up, wearing the kimono. It combined with his pierced ear and drooping mustache to make him look like some kind of exotic warlord. Kat watched as he went to a tray on an ornately carved Oriental dresser.

"I cooked breakfast," he said. Nathan turned and

winked at her. "Nothing as good as boiled frogs, but you'll like it."

Well, he was a domestic sort of warlord then. Kat sat up and straightened the dark, richly embroidered coverlet across her lap. Looking around at the luxurious Moroccan drapes anchored to the bedposts, she felt like the centerpiece of a sheik's tent.

"What ya got there?" she asked as he carried the tray to bed. "Some goat's milk and camel bacon?"

"Anything you want, gal. Anything for a naked woman who sits up with no clothes on." He settled beside her and carefully centered the simple glass tray, half on her thigh, half on his. Then he dipped a finger into a colorful ceramic bowl and dabbed her nipples with buttered grits.

"Now how am I gonna get that off?" she asked wryly.

"Hmmm. Let's see." He ducked his head and sucked each nipple for a few seconds. "Lookee there. All gone. And they're awake, too. Shows what a good breakfast can do."

This was terrible. She ought not to be thrilled with his attention. Kat smiled at him and fought back tears. He looked into her eyes and saw the evidence she couldn't hide.

"What are you afraid of, Katie?" He stroked her face with his fingertips.

She shook her head. "I'm havin' trouble adjusting. Us loners aren't used to being spoiled."

"You spoiled me yesterday." He lifted the corner of a blue silk sheet. "Remember?"

Oh, did she. They'd had to remake the bed because the sheets were on the floor. "We sure turned this into a wrestling ring."

He laughed. "No holds barred, no time limit."

"It was a great match."

His laughter died, and she saw the question in his eyes. He wanted to know why she'd gone into the den to hug her sash weight and cry. She wasn't going to tell him.

"Hey, what'd you do with my weird teddy bear?" Kat said lightly. "You know, the teddy with the rust on it?"

He smiled crookedly, but his eyes were still troubled. "It's on the nightstand."

She looked over and saw the thick sash weight resting between the phone and the lamp. "Thanks."

"Katie," he whispered. "Katie, don't be unhappy here. That's the last thing I want."

Katie. She couldn't help circling his neck with one arm and drawing him to her for a kiss. Afterward she tilted her forehead against his and murmured, "This is the hardest thing you could have asked me to do. To live here and take presents from you."

"I know," he said drolly. "It's hell."

"It is."

"You're my lover. It has nothing to do with our bargain about the land. I want you to have fun and do everything you ever daydreamed about doing. I'll give you whatever you like."

She exhaled raggedly and kissed him again. "Then give me the mining rights."

He drew back and eyed her. "Those mining rights are the only thing we're not gonna talk about, kid."

"Okay," she said pleasantly, and hoped her fingers didn't tremble when she lifted a piece of toast to her mouth.

But he wasn't fooled. "You'll forget and forgive," he assured her. "You're gonna be happy here."

She dropped the toast and shook her head. "Don't ask for that, Nathan. That's one thing I can't promise you."

"Don't need promises. Just need time." He lounged back on the bed's enormous pillows, put his hands behind his head, and said cheerfully, "Now if you want to feel like a slave, you can feed me."

Kat dug her fingers into a mound of scrambled eggs and cast a slant-eyed look at him.

He chuckled. "But since you're not a slave, you can do what you want."

She threw the eggs at him. They landed where the half-tied kimono exposed most of his chest. He yelped, then grew quiet as she pulled the garment open and cleaned the eggs up with her mouth. "I don't need promises. I just need time," she echoed between bites.

She dragged herself around her beautiful prison, wishing she'd get over the awkward feeling. She'd lived here for ten days. In nomad terms, that was a long time.

Kat roamed from room to room, absorbed with thoughts of how cheerful Nathan had been before he left that morning. He had to fly to New York on business, and he wouldn't be back until tomorrow. He hadn't asked her to go with him.

Kat wondered if she weren't good enough to take to New York. She reminded herself that Nathan was proud of her, and now that she knew the kind of family background he'd come from—grandpa an alcoholic, father a worthless drifter—she had even less reason to worry that he looked down on her.

But a question kept nagging at her—Was he proud of her, or had he brought her here to spruce her up so that he _could_ be proud of her? Hell, he'd sent the Mustang to a body shop so she'd have to drive the new Toyota she'd picked out. Maybe he wanted her retooled, too.

Kat went to her purse, got out a personal calendar book, and checked to see where the Wild Women of Wrestling tour was at the moment. Tonight in Jacksonville, Florida. She noted the name of the motel the tour always used in Jacksonville and placed a call to Muffie.

"Kat, when ya comin' back?" Muffie bellowed.

"Don't know." Kat tested her ankle and felt a little guilty because it was completely healed. "What's cooking?"

"We need ya, we need ya. Mary sprained her knee last night in Orlando. She's out for a couple of days."

Kat wiped a sweaty palm on the leg of her new designer jeans. Then she looked at the palm a moment and realized that she'd been hoping for an excuse to go back where she belonged, if only for a night.

"I'll be there as soon as I can get a plane."

"You got money for flying?"

"Sure." Kat shut her eyes. *Nathan wants me to be happy. Well, this makes me happy.* She'd leave word with his administrative assistant so that he'd know where she'd gone.

If Nathan was really proud of her the way she was, he wouldn't mind.

"Ladies and gentlemen, tonight we've got the grudge match of the summer! The one wrestling fans all over the Southeast have been waiting for! Five weeks ago Lady Savage, that mountain of female violence, injured the lovely Princess Talana in a despicable show of unsportsmanlike behavior! Tonight Princess Talana returns for the first time to wreak revenge on Lady Savage! And now, here she is—that vicious Valkyrie, Lady Savage!"

The crowd hissed and booed. Muffie slapped Kat on the shoulder. "This is gonna be a classic, kid, a classic."

Kat adjusted her warbonnet and grinned. "Just remember that you're supposed to win and I'm supposed to get hurt again—but not really hurt this time, okay?"

Muffie gave her a thumbs-up. Then, cone breasts quivering, she slung the entrance curtains aside and marched down the aisle to the ring, her spear held aloft.

Kat sadly touched the garish stripes of war paint on her cheeks. She was a Cherokee at heart, and that was all that mattered.

"And now let's give a big Jacksonville welcome to that powerful Pocahontas, that incredible Indian, that cute Cherokee, Princess Talana!"

Kat ran to the ring, leapt to the edge as usual, and waved to the cheering crowd. "Hi ya, folks!" No more Tonto talk. That was one thing she'd never do again.

Suddenly Muffie's hands latched around her throat. "Kill squaw!"

As she turned and belted Muffie right between the cones Kat heard the announcer scream, "Five seconds into the match and they've already gone berserk!"

Kat almost grinned. It was good to be in charge again.

Nathan reached the auditorium—one of those concrete relics from the thirties, with gargoyles on the outside and lots of cracking plaster on the inside—in time to see Kat's entrance.

He almost groaned aloud. Was she so damned desperate to get away from him that she'd go back to this humiliating life? He made his way down to the front. Since this was a weeknight the place was only half-full, so he managed to find an empty seat in the third row.

Nathan stared hard at her and hoped that she'd spot him in the audience, but she didn't. He sat on the edge of his folding chair, his fingers digging into the dark trousers he wore with a white pullover.

He hadn't been in New York at all. He'd been up in North Carolina, talking Grandpa Sam into giving him Kat's medallion. Nathan wanted to present it to her himself, when the time was right. Grandpa Sam, being a romantic, had agreed. He'd just finished translating it, and he understood that Nathan was the man who was meant to love Kat.

But now this. Nathan cursed under his breath. He wouldn't lose her to this carnival, no matter how much she despised what he planned to do with her family's land.

"Hi ya, folks!" she yelled to the crowd.

Well, at least she'd given up the dime store Indian talk. But he winced inwardly at the silly face paint and gaudy warbonnet, at the tight leather top and fringed miniskirt which revealed too much of her to the men around him.

"Swing that wampum, Princess!' someone called.

Lady Savage grabbed her and she punched in retaliation. Lady Savage dragged her into the ring and they went down in a heap of flesh—most of it belonging to Lady Savage.

There was a giant redneck next to Nathan, his tractor cap emblazoned with the bottom half of a woman's bikini-clad body and an obscene slogan. He stood up, cupped his hands around a mouth full of gold-capped teeth, and yelled, "Shake that booty, Princess!"

Nathan stood also, swung the man toward him, and laid a fist into the mother lode.

There was general chaos after that, and Nathan was dimly aware of the redneck's fist crunching into his face and of the man's slow, pained collapse as he got a knee in the groin. A small, gleeful war broke out among the men around them.

The security guards showed up, some of them carrying billy clubs. Nathan went down seeing stars after a club slammed into the back of his head. With people stepping on him, he was only vaguely aware when someone grabbed his arms.

"Help me pull, Muffie!"

A second later he was out of the chaos, feeling the cool concrete floor of the auditorium under him, his head in a soft, sweaty lap. He'd recognize that lap anywhere.

"Katie, gal," he said groggily, trying to blink away the blackness over his eyes. "You didn't think they'd hang an old buzzard like me, did ya?"

That didn't make sense. He couldn't figure out why, because his head was still celebrating the Fourth of July, but he heard Kat say desperately, "He's addled. We've gotta get him to a hospital."

That jarred him back to reality. "Hate hospitals," he muttered. "Everything's too clean." The blackness receded and he gazed up into Kat's face.

"Are you in there, Nathan?" she asked in a small, ragged voice. She bent over him, tears smearing her war paint, her hand stroking his forehead with quick, worried movements. For a moment she searched his eyes, then exhaled with relief.

"I came to get you out of all this," he said weakly, and shut his eyes against a wave of dizziness. He felt her small, gentle hand dabbing a cloth under his nose. "Bleeding?" he asked.

"Yeah," she whispered. "Like a stuck pig. A handsome stuck pig, though."

"I started the fight."

"Why?"

"Jerk said something . . . ugly about you."

Her hand stopped moving. "And you were ashamed."

"Not ashamed." He tried to shake his head. "Always take care of you. Always have. Always will."

She called his name softly and kissed him on the forehead. "Let's go home, sweetcakes, and I'll take care of you."

It was long past midnight before they got back to Atlanta. She kept one arm around his waist and watched him anxiously as she guided him through his penthouse to the bedroom.

"You walk okay for an addled man," Kat noted.

He nodded, peered at her over the bandage covering his scraped nose, and smiled gingerly. "Thanks."

After he lay down, Kat pulled his clothes off and brought him a handful of ice wrapped in a washcloth. She sat beside him and held the ice to his face. "What am I gonna do with you? You can't go around beating people up on my account."

His voice was muffled, but firm. "I won't be fighting again because you won't be wrestling."

Kat counted to ten. After all, he was hurt and addled. "That an order, master?"

He pulled the ice pack off his face and looked at her. "I never got the feeling that you like to wrestle."

"I like to work. I like to be around people. I can't sit here alone all day."

"Go to college."

Kat shook her head. "College is one more thing you'd have to pay for. I want to wrestle—just part-time, okay? You keep saying that you want me to do what makes me happy."

"Not wrestling."

"So it *is* an order," she said grimly, tingling with anger.

"Yep. If there's no other way to stop you from being a proud fool, then it's an order. Here's another one. Go down to Georgia State University tomorrow and get a catalogue and admission forms. I want you enrolled in college."

She got up from the bed and gazed at him with barely concealed fury. "I won't do it."

"You will do it. Or you won't ever get your medallion."

Kat listened in amazement as he explained that her legacy from great-aunt Dove was now in his possession. "How'd you con that sweet old man out of it?" she demanded.

"That's a secret between Grandpa Sam and me. It was no con."

Her teeth clenched, she said, "Don't ever tell me I'm free to do what I want again. And don't ever try to make me think I'm not your slave." She backed away a few steps, clasped her hands, and bowed low.

He threw the ice pack onto the floor. "Dammit, stop that!"

"You won't need me in bed tonight, master. You're in no shape to enjoy me. Your nose is bleeding again, for one thing. Can I have the night off and sleep in the guest room?"

"No! I want you in this bed now!" His face was contorted with pain from yelling. He looked miserable, and a stab of concern nearly dissolved Kat's anger.

So this was what it meant to love someone. Even when she wanted to strangle him, she didn't want him to hurt.

"Naked?" she asked.

"Buck-naked! If it's good enough for me—"

His eyes flickered shut and he winced from pain. Kat dropped her jeans, T-shirt, and underwear, retrieved the ice pack, and crawled into bed beside him.

"Just keep your mouth closed, Chatham, and maybe I won't punch you myself." She pressed the pack to his face, bending close to him with her bare breasts flattened on his shoulder.

He raised the hand next to her, fumbled for a moment, then finally grabbed one of her knees and held it tightly. "I'm trying to do what's best for you."

"I said keep quiet," she ordered. Kat reached across him, turned out the bedside lamp, then gently pulled his head to her breasts and held him. "Go to sleep. I'll keep the ice pack on your face for a while."

"I'm trying to do what's . . . best," he repeated, but his voice was drugged with pain and exhaustion.

Then love me, she told him silently.

The phone rang. Good, something to do. There were about a dozen extensions in Nathan's apartment;

half the fun was just deciding which one to use. She turned Geraldo Rivera off in the den and went to the jungle room to pick up the phone there.

"Chatham residence."

"It's Echo."

Kat froze. "Yeah?"

"Kat, are you with Nathan Chatham?"

There was no point in bluffing. "I'm with him," Kat said wearily.

"Tess and Erica tried to find you on the wrestling tour. My grandpa finished translating Dove's papers, and there are a lot of things you need to know."

Kat breathed in shallow gulps. "They tried to find me?"

"And they couldn't. Because you never went back to the tour, did you?"

"No," Kat said, defeated.

"So—"

"They suspected me and Nathan all along, didn't they."

"Yes."

"How'd you trace me here?"

Echo sighed. "Give Jeopard Surprise twenty-four hours and he could probably find Jimmy Hoffa and Amelia Earhart."

Her knees weak, Kat sank onto a chair. "So they think I double-crossed 'em?"

Echo's voice was regretful. "Yes, they do."

Kat shut her eyes and thought, *Now I'm going to lose my family, too.*

When he got home that night Nathan found her sitting in the dusky light of the garden room, dressed in a beautiful gray jumpsuit and matching pumps, her hair pulled up in a sleek braided coil, her face utterly composed and unfathomable.

"Good day?" she asked, and got up to kiss him.

"Yeah."

She hugged him—no, she let him hug her, and as soon as he loosened his grip she moved away, not with distaste, just not particularly interested in being near him.

"Hope you're hungry," she said pleasantly. "I called one of the restaurants over at Lenox Square and ordered everything short of a side of beef. Real gourmet." She chuckled. "Everything has parsley on it. Head for the dining room and I'll cart it to ya."

"You okay?" he asked, sliding his hand around her arm to halt her easy stroll out of the room.

"Sure." But though she looked up at him with a smile, her eyes squinted as if in pain.

Nathan took her face between his hands and rubbed his thumbs across her lower lids. They felt hot and a little puffy. "Have you been crying?" he murmured.

"Nah. I sat in the Jacuzzi too long, that's all. Makes me bloat." She grinned at him.

He wasn't sure he believed her, but he didn't press for details. Nathan chucked her under the chin. "We've got to find something to keep you out of the Jacuzzi so much. Did you go down to Georgia State today?"

She shrugged. "Sure. I got a catalogue. No hurry. You tired of me already?"

"Nope, but whatd'ya think I brought you here for? Just to order food and look pretty and ravish me every time I come home?"

The smile that stayed on her mouth didn't do a thing to hide the discomfort creeping deeper into her eyes. "Whatever you want."

Frustration jabbed at him. "I want you to act like this is your home and I'm your friend."

"Okay. I can act that way."

He made a growling sound of disgust. "I don't mean *act*, dammit."

"Then tell me how I'm supposed to *feel*. I've never lived with anybody before, except when I was married."

Nathan said loudly, "Well, pretend that we're married."

She trembled and stepped back from him. "Nope," she said in a soft, fierce voice. " 'Cause we're not married and we're never gonna be married. I'm going to stay here as long as you want me, and when you say leave, I'm leavin'."

Stunned by her vehement words, he gazed at her silently and watched her struggle to regain her calm façade. The fact that she was able to do it nearly tore him apart, and dull fury poured into the wound.

"If I want an actress I'll hire one," he told her.

"If you want dinner you better come get it," she answered, and left the room.

A minute later, after he got his anguish under control enough to speak normally, he walked into the kitchen to talk. This was not the Kat Gallatin he knew, the woman who had a deep and true need for him.

She stood at a counter putting baked fish on a platter. When she heard his footsteps on the tile she turned, smiled carefully, and said, "I'll learn how to cook, if you say so."

Nathan halted, his control evaporating in light of her continued nonchalance. She just wanted to do her part and be left alone. In front of an audience she could play Princess Talana and fake fear, anger, or pain. In front of him she could play his happy lover and fake contentment.

"Take the night off," he said with sick disappointment that made his tone cruel. "I'll go out to get dinner—and anything else I need."

He left the apartment with the memory of her haunted eyes as his only victory.

Nathan had walked less than a block from the building when the fat yellow cab made a U-turn across three lanes of city traffic and bounced off the sidewalk in its careening journey toward him.

It screeched to a stop too close to his legs, and the dull agony simmering inside him exploded into violence. Nathan vaulted around the front of the cab and jerked the driver's door open.

"Get outta there, you SOB!"

"Get in this car, you SOB," a female voice demanded.

"Immediately," another said.

Nathan bent down and looked past a terrified driver into the back. Tess and Erica leaned toward him, poised like two dangerous tigers just waiting for an excuse to pounce.

"We came to see our cousin," Erica said.

"But you'll do nicely," Tess finished. "Get in."

Nathan gave them a grim smile, nodded, and went to the front passenger side. He was ready for another good fight.

Two beers, too little sleep, then when she did sleep, rotten dreams. Kat woke the next morning with a pounding headache and a thick cloak of misery around her.

She dragged herself off the couch, looked down at the wrinkled mess of her jumpsuit, and turned around in a circle, feeling groggy and trying to put the world right.

Her hair was in her eyes—that was part of the problem. She pawed it aside, then realized that it had been braided atop her head when she'd gone to sleep. Now it was undone, and someone had brushed it very gently so she wouldn't wake up.

She wobbled in place, her heart twisting, then called out plaintively, "Nathan?" She had a desperate need to feel his arms around her.

Kat hurried through the rooms, bumping into things because her head hurt and she was upset. He wasn't anywhere, and the closet door stood open.

Kat stared at it and couldn't bring herself to see if his clothes were gone.

Aw, why would he leave his own place? He'd tell her to leave. But fear churned inside her as she went back to the den. Now she was awake enough to notice that her hairbrush lay on the teakwood coffee table by the couch. Under the brush was a sheet of Auraria, Inc., letterhead with a handwritten note from Nathan.

"*Kat.* The mining rights are yours, now—yours and your cousins'. I found out some things that put the family feud in a different light. Tess and Erica are staying at the Peachtree Plaza, waiting to see you this morning. Don't worry. They know the truth now, and they're proud of you. Our deal's done. I'm going to Surador. You're free, Katie."

Kat lay back on the couch, tears scalding her eyes. "Not free," she whispered. "Just alone."

Ten

Tess and Erica grabbed her duffel bag, then drew her into their hotel room and hugged her. She immediately began to cry. "You don't hate me?" Kat asked.

"For trying to rescue the land?" Erica asked, sniffling.

"And falling in love with a sweet man like Nathan?" Tess added.

"How do you know I'm in love with him?"

They led her to a couch and sat down on either side of her. "We suspected it that day at the homeplace."

"We *know* how people look at each other when they're in love."

"We're really quite expert on it, both of us."

Kat smiled at them wanly. Nathan didn't love her, but she couldn't bring herself to say so at the moment. "Why did he give us the mining rights back?"

"Because he loves you."

"And because it's the only honorable thing to do, now that he's seen the other side of the Chatham-Gallatin feud."

Kat wiped her eyes and looked from Tess to Erica in surprise. "Another side?"

"The family history Dove wrote down. Grandpa Sam finished translating it," Erica explained. "We told Nathan. He said it was too detailed and made too much sense not to be true."

She took Kat's right hand. Tess took her left one. Kat looked back and forth between them, scrutinizing the solemn excitement in their eyes. "What did Dove say?"

Tess smiled. "Your great-grandfather Holt didn't shoot Nathaniel Chatham, but he was a prime suspect because everyone knew the Gallatins despised Nathaniel."

"Nathaniel was the Union officer who captured Justis in the Indian Territory during the war," Erica reminded Kat. "His men took everything the Gallatins owned. The only way Katherine could save Justis from being executed was to bribe one of Chatham's men with the three medallions. After Justis escaped, Chatham found out about the bribe and confiscated the medallions."

"That's what the big scandal was about," Tess noted. Chatham was accused of taking part in the bribe, because he also had a gold nugget that belonged to Justis."

Kat frowned, trying to sort everything out. "So Chatham kept our medallions?"

Tess nodded. "At least that's what everyone thought. It couldn't be proved. But it's why Holt was accused of ambushing him, a few years after the war. The Chatham family started a campaign to have Holt arrested and tried—"

"And for a Cherokee, that meant automatic death," Erica explained. "So Holt became an outlaw. He had to."

Kat looked at her askance. "So he *did* go around blasting people?"

"No, he went around robbing every business the Chathams owned. Dove said he never shot anyone except in self-defense, not in all the years he tormented the Chathams."

"Until finally they sent a small army of U.S. marshals after him," Tess interjected. "Holt had a log fortress hidden in the hills. The marshals found it, and when Holt refused to surrender, they burned the place to the ground."

Kat felt Erica's and Tess's hands squeezing hers tighter. Erica looked at her sympathetically. "But the horrible thing was, Holt wasn't there. His wife was there, and his five children, and they'd lied to the marshals to throw them off Holt's track."

Kat winced. "So that's why Dove and my grandfather Joshua were born so late in Holt's life. They were his second family. Poor Great-grandfather."

Tess nodded. "Right. And after that, Holt waged war on the marshals *and* the Chathams."

"Finally, thirty years after Nathaniel was shot, a witness came forward and said that Holt wasn't responsible."

"So Great-grandpa was cleared of the murder charge, and he turned peaceful?" Kat asked.

Both cousins nodded. "But he never forgot that the Chathams had his mother's medallions," Erica said. "When he was an old man he and Eli, Nathaniel's son, tried to call a truce. Eli said he'd give the medallions back if Holt would sign over the mining rights to the Blue Song land in Georgia."

"So that's why Great-grandpa did it," Kat said softly. "But why'd he and Eli have a gunfight years later?"

"They just plain couldn't stand each other," Tess said, imitating Kat's sideways twang.

"So they killed each other. Dove inherited the Blue Song land and the medallions."

Kat sighed. "She got Eli's married son, Micah, too."

Erica straightened proudly. "Well, I believe in Dove.

I live in her house now, you know, and I think that she told the truth about everything, including Micah."

"So what'd she say?"

"Oh, they were having an affair, all right," Tess admitted. "But they'd been in love for years before Micah married someone else. Eli wouldn't let his son marry a Gallatin—he threatened to disinherit him, and apparently Micah was *not* gallant enough to forgo money to marry Dove."

"Dove made the mistake of still loving him," Erica noted. "But I think we can forgive her for loving too deeply, can't we?"

Kat nodded. "Then she got pregnant—"

"And she went to England to save everyone some grief."

"But Micah's wife learned the truth, anyway. End of story."

Kat looked at her cousins with tears that matched their own. "But what happened after Dove's baby and her English husband died?"

"Dove came back to the States and settled on the reservation in North Carolina."

"Did Dove say anything about Justis and Katherine? I guess they'd passed on before she was born."

"Yes, but she wrote down what Holt told her," Tess said softly. "The only reason Justis had to have a white wife was to keep Katherine's land for her. In the state of Georgia any man who married a Cherokee was considered a Cherokee, too. He would have lost everything including the Blue Song land."

"And Amarintha Parnell needed a respectable husband," Erica said, "who was willing to give a respectable name to a baby that wasn't his."

Kat sank her head in her hands. "So Justis kept up a show for Katlanicha's sake."

There was a knock at the door. "Must be the pot of tea I ordered," Tess murmured, as she crossed the room. "We can certainly use it."

The waiter tromped inside, loaded with a full tray, and immediately tripped over Kat's duffel bag. As everyone tried to help him up, he grimaced.

"Are you hurt?" Tess inquired.

"My foot hit something *hard* in that bag. I think I broke it."

"Your foot?" Erica asked.

"No. Whatever's in the end of the bag."

"My sash weight!" Kat cried. She pulled the bag open and dug clothes out of it desperately. "It was so rusty and frail. And it's hollow, Nathan said. If it's broken—not today, please, not today, I can't take it—"

Kat stuck one hand into the bag and hit a pile of metal fragments. Swallowing tightly, she finally managed to say, "It's broken into about a hundred little pieces."

"There are two dozen more of those weights back at the homeplace," Tess said gently.

Erica hugged Kat's shoulders. "That's right."

But this is the first one Nathan and I found together. Crying silently, Kat pulled a handful of broken metal out of the bag.

The coins caught the light and held it—golden, ageless, and shimmering with dreams that had finally come true.

Kat had a quarter of a million dollars, her share of the modern market value for 850 gold coins minted before 1810. Hidden inside twenty-five hollow iron sash weights, the rare coins were expected to send collectors all over the world into a frenzy. There were an additional thirty coins, but each of the Gallatin cousins kept ten for sentimental reasons.

Nathan put the newspaper down and wished he hadn't gotten this news on his first day back from Surador. He'd lived for this day, hoping that time and restored mining rights had helped Kat forget that he'd tried to manipulate her into staying with him.

And that he had every intention of manipulating her again.

Nathan smiled grimly. The medallion would help him win her. He was the only person who knew what it said, who knew what great-great-grandmother Katlanicha had been waiting all these years to tell them.

"*Listen!* His name is Tahchee. He is adopted of the deer clan. His body, I take it. His flesh, I take it. His heart, I take it. Bind his soul to mine, never to turn away. I am *da-nitaka*, standing in his soul. It was decided long ago."

She'd said those words several times a day for the past three weeks. If anything could make Nathan come here on her terms, they would. The conniving rogue was home from Surador, and if he wanted his gold nugget back, he'd have to beg for it—and bring her medallion to trade.

If he didn't, she'd have to think of another way to get him to come to her.

The brisk September air made her glad she'd donned a long-sleeved work shirt, plus knee-high socks under her jeans and Reeboks. A breeze carried whispers of fall through the trees, and a hawk swung overhead, black against a deep blue sky. Kat watched it quietly.

The hawk floated for a moment as if suspended in time, and then glided out of sight.

Carrying rough sketches of her house, Kat shut the door of the camper she'd rented and walked along the ridge to the old homesite. It was cleared now, the crumbling fieldstone foundation showing where the Blue Song house had stood and also showing, with the blackened rocks, that it had burned the day the soldiers came.

She, Tess, and Erica figured that even Katlanicha and Justis hadn't known about the sash weights full of gold coins. Justis would have had plenty of opportunity to gather them during his trips back to Georgia to visit Amarintha Parnell, and he surely wouldn't have left the sash weights lying around on open ground, thinking that no one would steal them.

Obviously Katlanicha's parents had hidden the gold coins when they built their house, before their children were born.

So the land was a legacy from Katlanicha Blue Song, who became Katherine Gallatin but never forgot her Cherokee homeplace; and the coins were a legacy from the Blue Song family.

Kat stood in the center of the old homesite, thinking how the house was going to rise from the ashes like a phoenix, restored as close to the way it'd looked before as she could determine, though maybe it'd be a little bigger—there had to be plenty of room for Tess and Erica to visit with their families. They expected to build places here someday, but for now she'd be the only Gallatin on the property.

Well, not the only one, but the only flesh-and-blood one. Okay, so she really didn't believe in ghosts—she simply liked to think she wasn't alone here. Nothing odd about that.

Kat shut her eyes and pictured the house finished before Christmas. Her first Christmas in her old home. Her old home?

"*Osiyo,* Katlanicha."

She dropped her sketches and whirled, searching the woods. Nathan, dressed in his buckskin breeches, moccasins, and a light gray sweater the color of his eyes, was leaning against an oak, his arms crossed nonchalantly over his chest as he watched her.

Her medallion gleamed on the end of the long gold chain he wore.

Her heart racing, Kat pulled the chain with the gold nugget out of her shirt. "*Osiyo*, you sly-footed hellion."

He smiled slowly and walked toward her, every step a measured enticement telling her that he read the welcome in her eyes. But this feud wasn't over.

Nathan stopped too close for her comfort and said in a droll voice, "You're a rich little hummingbird now. You've got money, you've got your land, you've got your home—and nobody can ever hurt it again. That's what Katherine and Justis intended. You don't need to know what your medallion says. Everything's settled."

Kat shook her head sadly. "You and me aren't settled. You left me. You didn't want me anymore. And now I don't know what I expected when I saw you again, but it looks like you came here only to make me feel bad."

"Nope. I gave you freedom so you'd forget what I'd done to you. Then I came here today to tell you that you can't forget me."

Feeling a little dazed by the way he was looking at her, she took a step back. "You wanted me to forget."

He stepped forward. "Nope. You can't forget. You'll never forget." Suddenly he was touching her, slipping one arm around her, pulling her to him while he nestled a hand into her hair. "You'll always need me, Katie."

Katie. His hand. Her hair. Oh no. Kat shut her eyes and put her arms around his neck, then raised her mouth and caught his in a long, spellbound kiss.

She rested her forehead against his shoulder and felt the swift movement of his chest, the harsh grip of his hands on her, her own body trembling. "Needing and having are two different things," she whispered.

"No."

Tilting her head back, she looked at him wretchedly. "I'm going to college. I've already talked to the people at the one in Gold Ridge. They say all I have to do is take some catch-up courses first."

"Yeah? So?"

Kat frowned. Was he dense? "So maybe I'll be educated enough for you."

"Good God, who said you weren't?"

She studied him closely. "Are you ashamed of me for being so low-rent? Tell the truth."

With a soft groan of dismay he took her face between his hands. "You're not low-rent, sweetheart. And if I were any prouder of you, I'd be hard to live with."

Giddy and confused, she said solemnly, "You *were* hard to live with in Atlanta. I didn't know you anymore."

"Is that why you stopped wanting me?"

She cried out sadly. "I didn't know how to treat you. All those gifts, all that fancy stuff . . . I just wanted my old Nathan back, the one who roamed the woods and took buck-naked baths outdoors."

"I can manage that for you."

She pulled away, shaking her head and sweeping a hand around her. "You'd have to live here with me."

"Best invitation I've heard in years. I accept."

His eyes gleamed like old silver as he grabbed her hand. Without a word he pulled her along beside him as he headed for the front of the ridge.

Openmouthed, Kat stared at him, wondering what gave his eyes such a compelling purpose and set his mouth in a knowing little smile.

He stopped at the edge of the ridge, gazed out over the valley as if mesmerized by its beauty, then rested his fingertips on her medallion and looked at her the same way he'd looked at the valley.

"Do you want to know what your medallion says?" he asked softly.

Kat caught her breath. "Oh *yes.*"

He shut his eyes for a moment, then locked his gaze to hers. His fingertips caressed the Cherokee symbols. "Taken from the land, given back to the land, this gold will bring us home."

His eyes never leaving Kat's, Nathan turned the medallion and touched the symbols on the other side. "I will know him by the gold over his heart."

Kat shook her head, puzzled. Nathan lifted the gold nugget from her chest. "This belonged to Justis."

She grasped lightly and clung to him with both hands. Kat looked down at the nugget he cupped reverently in his palm. "This belonged to Justis? This is the nugget your great-great-grandpa took from him."

"Not 'took from him,' " Nathan corrected gently. "Justis gave it to him to send to Katie after he was executed. Justis didn't expect to escape." Nathan paused. "This nugget's stayed in my family over a hundred years. I've worn it all my life."

Kat looked up at him and asked in a small, awed voice, "I will know him by the gold over his heart. Are you asking me to believe—"

"I'm just asking you to marry me, Katie."

She quivered with emotion, took his face between her hands, and searched his face until she knew she wasn't imagining what she saw there. "That night when I asked you to make a deal on the mining rights, I said that I loved you," Kat whispered. "You didn't believe me. Will you believe me now?"

His voice was gruff. "I'll believe you. Say it again for me, Katie."

"I love you, Nathan." She swayed against him, and he held her tightly. "And I'll marry you."

"Good. I love you, too." He kissed her, then murmured against her lips, "That sounds so right I know I've said it before." He chuckled hoarsely. "Maybe I've just thought it a lot."

"Maybe," she agreed. "But I've been waiting forever to hear it."

His smile was dear and familiar. "I knew it would be like this someday."

She saw past and future and an eternity of promises in his eyes. *Someday* had arrived.

THE EDITOR'S CORNER

Get ready for a month chockfull of adventure and romance! In October our LOVESWEPT heroes are a bold and dashing group, and you'll envy the heroines who win their hearts.

Starting off the month, we have **HOT TOUCH**, LOVESWEPT #354. Deborah Smith brings to life a dreamy hero in rugged vet Paul Belue. When Caroline Fitzsimmons arrives at Paul's bayou mansion to train his pet wolf for a movie, she wishes she could tame the male of her species the way she works her magic with animals. The elegant and mysterious Caroline fascinates Paul and makes him burn for her caresses, and when he whispers "Chere" in his Cajun drawl, he melts her resistance. A unique and utterly sensual romance, **HOT TOUCH** sizzles!

Your enthusiastic response to Gail Douglas's work has thrilled us all and has set Gail's creative juices flowing. Her next offering is a quartet of books called *The Dreamweavers*. Hop onboard for your first romantic journey with Morgan Sinclair in LOVESWEPT #355, **SWASHBUCKLING LADY.** Morgan and her three sisters run The Dreamweavers, an innovative travel company. And you'll be along for the ride to places exotic as each falls in love with the man of her dreams.

When hero Cole Jameson spots alluring pirate queen Morgan, he thinks he's waltzed into an old Errol Flynn movie! But Morgan enjoys her role as Captain of a restored brigantine, and she plays it brilliantly for the tourists of Key West. In Morgan, Cole finds a woman who's totally guileless, totally without pretense—and he doesn't know how to react to her honesty, especially since he can't disclose his own reasons for being in Key West. Intrigued and infuriated by Cole's elusive nature, Morgan thinks she's sailing in unchar-
(continued)

tered waters. We guarantee you'll love these two charming characters—or we'll walk the plank!

One of our favorite writing teams, Adrienne Staff and Sally Goldenbaum return with **THE GREAT AMERICAN BACHELOR,** LOVESWEPT #356. Imagine you're on the worst blind date of your life . . . and then you're spirited away on a luxury yacht by a handsome hunk known in the tabloids as the Great American Bachelor! Cathy Stevenson is saved—literally—by Michael Winters when he pulls her from the ocean, and her nightmare turns into a romantic dream. Talk about envying a heroine! You'll definitely want to trade places with Cathy in this story of a modern day Robinson Crusoe and his lady love!

Peggy Webb will take you soaring beyond the stars with **HIGHER THAN EAGLES,** LOVESWEPT #357. From the first line you'll be drawn into this powerfully evocative romance.

A widow with a young son, Rachel Windham curses the fates who've brought the irresistible pilot Jacob Donovan back from his dangerous job of fighting oil rig fires. Jacob stalks her relentlessly, demanding she explain why she'd turned her back on him and fled into marriage to another man, and Rachel can't escape—not from the mistakes of the past, nor the yearning his mere presence stirs in her. Peggy does a superb job in leading Rachel and Jacob full circle through their hurts and disappointments to meet their destiny in each other's arms.

Next in our LOVESWEPT lineup is #358, **FAMILIAR WORDS** by Mary Kay McComas. Mary Kay creates vividly real characters in this sensitive love story between two single parents.

Beth Simms is mortified when her little boy, Scotty, calls ruggedly handsome Jack Reardan "daddy" during the middle of Sunday church services. She knows that every male Scotty sees is "daddy," but
(continued)

there's something different about this man whose wicked teasing makes her blush. Jack bulldozes Beth's defenses and forges a path straight to her heart. You won't want to miss this lively tale, it's peppered with humor and emotion as only Mary Kay can mix them!

Barbara Boswell finishes this dazzling month with **ONE STEP FROM PARADISE**, LOVESWEPT #359. Police officer Lianna Novak is furious when she's transferred to Burglary, but desire overwhelms her fury when she meets Detective Michael Kirvaly. Urged on by wild, dangerous feelings for Michael, Lianna risks everything by falling in love with her new partner. Michael's undeniable attraction to Lianna isn't standard operating procedure, but the minute the sultry firecracker with the sparkling eyes approached his desk, he knew he'd never let her go—even if he had to handcuff her to him and throw away the key. Barbara will really capture your heart with this delightful romance.

We're excited and curious to know what you think of our new look, so do write and tell us. We hope you enjoy it!

Best wishes from the entire LOVESWEPT staff,
Sincerely,

Carolyn Nichols

Carolyn Nichols
Editor
LOVESWEPT
Bantam Books
666 Fifth Avenue
New York, NY 10103

NEW!

Handsome Book Covers Specially Designed To Fit Loveswept Books

Our new French Calf Vinyl book covers come in a set of three great colors— royal blue, scarlet red and kachina green.

Each 7" × 9½" book cover has two deep vertical pockets, a handy sewn-in bookmark, and is soil and scratch resistant.

To order your set, use the form below.